Secrets of Silvercreek

To Ryllis, enjoy,

Roger Hart
Proverbs 18:24

Secrets of Silvercreek

Roger M. Hart

Copyright © 2018 Roger M. Hart

ISBN # 10:1721034501
ISBN# 13: 978-1721034505

All rights reserved. No part of this book may be reproduced or transmitted in any form or by any means, electronic or mechanical, including photocopying, recording, or by any information storage and retrieval system, without permission in writing from the copyright owner.
This is a work of fiction. Names, characters, places and incidents either are the product of the author's imagination or are used fictitiously, and any resemblance to any actual persons, living or dead, events or locales is entirely coincidental.

All Bible quotations are taken from the King James Version.
Other quotations are given credit in the author's note page.
This book was printed in the United States of America.

Rev. Date June 2018
To order more copies log into:
Createspace.com, or
Amazon Books.

Dedication

Secrets of Silvercreek is dedicated to all of the young people and men and women of Christian County, Kentucky who have lived and loved their county.

Other books by the author include:

"Poems From The Heart"

"Joys and Tears"

Little House By The Edge Of The Woods, series

"Benjamin and the Fredrickson Girls"
"Roland and the Crankenbeal Family"
"Patrick and Olivia"
"The Star of Bailly School"
"A Different World"

A stand alone book
"Joy's Return"

"Secrets of Silvercreek,"

Contents

Chapter 1.   Bettie's First Day at School
Chapter 2.   An Attitude
Chapter 3.   Tight As Glue
Chapter 4.   An Eagle's Nest
Chapter 5.   Heap Big Braves Learn To Cook
Chapter 6.   Pembroke's First Motor Car
Chapter 7.   A Man Called Moses
Chapter 8.   The Lookout Tower
Chapter 9.   Whispering Pete
Chapter 10. Buried Silver
Chapter 11. Home Visits
Chapter 12. Bettie and the Fly.
Chapter 13. The Silvercreek Cave
Chapter 14. Almost A Lady
Chapter 15. Abigail
Chapter 16. Mr. Browning
Chapter 17. Old Baccer Worm
Chapter 18. Billy
Chapter 19. The Eighth Grade
Chapter 20. Graduation
Chapter 21. A Shrine
Chapter 22. Am I A Jew
Chapter 23. Dark Tobacco Problems
Chapter 24. All Tingly Feeling
Chapter 25. Their Beloved Bettie
Chapter 26. Really Alone
Chapter 27. Belinda's Anguish
Chapter 28. Princess and The Wildflower

Prologue

Belinda thought only one thing kept Bettie from being the perfect child. A perfect companion to a young mother while her husband, John, was away for years serving his country as an Army officer. But try as she might, she *couldn't* keep Bettie at home with her as much as she wanted. She, as most mothers, wanted to teach her daughter how to sew, cook, and keep a house for her husband to be. What motherhood and being a wife meant to a young girl.

But from the time Bettie started school she ran and played with her two *best* and *only* friends Johnny Rivers and Clarence Clearwater. At six, Bettie along with Johnny and Clarence, started the first grade at Pembroke Elementary School, Pembroke, Kentucky.

That was the fall of 1905 when the boys first became Bettie's friend and started looking out for her, as if they were her brothers, guards, and only companions.

It started when Billy Johnson pestered Bettie the first day of school to get her attention. They became *knights* in shining armor to protect Bettie. From that day forward the threesome were bound together by an unseen, and sometimes exasperating, influence that no one else ever understood.

At a young age this threesome both unlocked and held the Secrets of Silvercreek.

Chapter One

September 1905, Pembroke, Kentucky

Bettie first met Johnny and Clarence on their first day of school at Pembroke Elementary School, Pembroke, Kentucky. Monday, September 4th, 1905. They were the, usual or unusual, whichever way a body chooses to look at things, small town boys of the day. She noticed both boys dressed the same way in bib overalls and checkered shirts.

At that age she had no idea the roll they would play in her life and how dependent she would be on them in their years growing up. Right then all she was interested in was getting thru the first day of school.

When she first looked at Johnny and Clarence she thought they might be twins or at least brothers. Their clothes were the same, their hair cut and combed the same, except Johnny had dark hair and Clarence had lighter almost sandy red hair. But later she found out they were both an only child; just as she was.

Bettie's mama had bought material at the General Store and made a new dress for her to wear on her first day of school. It was pale yellow with blue, green and orange butterflies all over; she helped pick it out.

Up until then she had been mama's little girl and never gave any thought about what other kids wore. She just wore the little girl clothes her mama made for her and that was that. As she dressed for her first day of school she thought her new dress looked extra pretty to start school in. Her mama brushed and curled her auburn hair to make her feel like she'd be the prettiest girl at school.

Being an only child she could understand why Johnny and Clarence were such close friends; having no other siblings to play with. Thru the years she often wondered if that was the secret that drew them all together. *True-blue, tight-as-glue,* was often said of those three kids.

On the first day of school she learned that Johnny's name was Johnny Rivers and Clarence was Clarence Clearwater. She thought they were funny names and the first chance she had she whispered to them, "Are you two Indians?"

"Naw, not anymore," was Johnny's only reply.

"My grandpa was an Indian," Clarence added.

Neither seemed to be big talkers.

It was their first day of school and their teacher, *Mrs. Claudia Pepperdine*, had dismissed school for an hour to eat their dinner and have playtime. It was during that hour of playtime their relationship first begin to bud. Johnny and Clarence were already friends but Bettie was a newcomer to Pembroke of the last year and hadn't made friends with them before.

But, from that very first day at school she was always thankful for Johnny and Clarence; even though they were *boys*. Being six years old though she didn't care whether they were a boy or girl; she just wanted friends.

As well as Johnny and Clarence a bully boy named Billy Johnson and another girl named Sadie Plummer had also started school that day. Five brand new first grade students for Mrs. Pepperdine that year.

****

She knew that day wasn't going to be one of her better days when she arrived at school and decided she didn't want to go to school after all. Being new and living at the edge of town had made making new friends difficult. Living at the edge of town like mama and she, and sometimes daddy did, meant there were no other families with children nearby. Today would be a big day for her to get to know other kids in town as well as get acquainted with school. Mama had taught her to recite the

ABC's, write them, and all the numbers. She could even count to 100.

"She was ready for school," her mama said.

Belinda hugged her that morning and first told her, "Your new dress makes you look so grown up." Then as if a second thought crept in she added,

"But you are still my little girl, how about if I walk you to school today?"

As they walked to school hand in hand she pretended to talk happily to her mama about school. She even noticed the large horse barns not far from the schoolhouse. But when they neared the schoolhouse and saw the teacher come to the door with a bell in her hand she knew it was almost time to go inside. The teacher looked around at all her students, smiled, and then gave the bell a shake telling everyone *playtime* was over and *school* had started.

She looked up at her mama and tried to smile but then her pretense broke. With eyes laden with tears she couldn't hold back any longer, she began to plead.

"Oh, Mama, I don't want to go to school. Please don't make me go. I don't know anyone here. You can teach me at home Mama, you are real smart, and I'll work real hard. You can teach me everything you know. Please Mama...*please don't make me go in!*"

"Honey, I can't be your school teacher. I am sure Mrs Pepperdine is a very nice lady and a very good teacher. I'll see that she knows your name and where she wants you to sit." "Would that make you feel better?" She smiled re-assuredly but somehow Bettie didn't feel any better.

Bettie didn't really think it would help but to her surprise she asked,

"Would you stay and sit with me? I think I could like going to school if you were here with me."

"I don't think Mrs. Pepperdine would want a mother to be in her school but let's go in and get you settled. Then we'll see if you want me to stay."

Bettie nodded slightly not at all sure she agreed with her mama but couldn't think of any more arguments to make.

With that little bit of progress Belinda and Bettie walked hand in hand into the *dreaded* school's interior. The other kid's eyes all fastened on her being led inside by her mama; some snickered. Belinda had expected as much but kept a hold of Bettie's hand as she walked to the front of Mrs. Pepperdine's desk.

"I'm Belinda Latimer, she said, and this is my daughter Bettie Latimer. Bettie was a little fearful of coming in alone so I told her I would see her settled... if that's ok."

Mrs. Pepperdine smiled and spoke to Belinda.

"I understand, Bettie isn't the first student I've had that was fearful of starting school. I've heard *almost* every excuse imaginable from a child not wanting to start school but I've yet to have one student die of fright."

Mrs. Pepperdine looked down at her, "Bettie, I'd like very much to get to know you and have you in my class. How about if I let you sit right here beside me today and we can get better acquainted."

With Bettie's slight nod Mrs. Pepperdine set a small straight backed chair beside her, much larger wooden-armed teacher's chair.

"There," she said looking at Bettie trying to calm her fears. "How is that?"

When Bettie climbed onto the chair Belinda breathed a sigh of relief. "What time will school be out today?" She asked.

"The first week I always let out at one o'clock." "After the first week it will be three o'clock. This week I just want the new students to get acquainted with being here."

"And," Mrs. Pepperdine leaned close to Belinda. "The first week I always let out early and walk the children over to the horse show building to get a closer look at the pretty horses still there after the horse show."

"I think Bettie would like that," Belinda replied.

Mrs. Pepperdine nodded then looked at our empty hands. "Did Bettie bring her lunch?"

Belinda's face turned a little pink as she shook her head no. "I completely forgot about fixing Bettie's lunch, I'm in worse shape than Bettie this morning. I guess it isn't hard to see that we Latimer women are a little emotional today."

"I'll go home and be right back with her lunch."

Mrs. Pepperdine only smiled and nodded her understanding at Belinda's flushed face.

When Belinda returned with Bettie's lunch all sign of any fear was gone. The girl named Sadie sat beside Bettie at Mrs. Pepperdine's desk looking at a book with pictures of bright colored worms. Belinda simply sat her lunch down, gave Mrs. Pepperdine a grateful wave and backed out the door before Bettie noticed.

****

Six years earlier:

For Belinda Eisenhall Latimer five years had gone by in the blink of an eye. First it had been marriage to John Latimer, his army enlistment, movement from Kansas to Kentucky, giving birth to her baby, and now five years later Bettie would soon be school age.

As she thought about the approaching school year she remembered waiting one afternoon for John to get home from the base at Camp Campbell, Belinda was ready with a question that had been heavy on her mind. It was more of a statement than a question but she hoped John would agree.

"John, I don't want Bettie growing up on a military base and be known as an Army brat, can we move away from the base, someplace where Bettie can grow up *safe* and be loved by all of our friends?"

It was a question she had been dwelling on for some time but didn't quite know how to approach John. He was a proud man and she never wanted him to think he had made the wrong decision to become an Army officer. Now-a-days he always seemed worried about war in Europe and the *incessant* training of new men had changed John from the young devil may care man she married. Yet, none the less, they had a child to think about, it wasn't just them anymore.

Her John had woven himself into the prestigious Eisenhall family of Topeka, Kansas by exercising patience. He waited and watched the family knowing he didn't have much to offer but his schooling and hopes of finding a good job. When the time was right, when the chances were better than good, he had made his move to get acquainted with Belinda; the second of the Eisenhall girls. Abigail came first, and then Belinda, Charming, and Deborah. The sight of them along with their mama, Etolia Henshaw Eisenhall, was enough to make any young man's heart flutter

Soon after John and Belinda married she knew she was in the *family way* and could hardly wait to tell him. He had enlisted in the Army at Fort Riley, Kansas, just a short distance from Topeka, and after his basic training was commissioned a Second Lieutenant. From there he was sent to Camp Campbell, Kentucky to help the new camp train young soldiers.

It had all happened like a whirlwind after they were married, when just a month after their marriage John enlisted at Fort Riley and after his basic training was finished he was sent to Kentucky. Belinda had lived all her life in Topeka and never thought of living elsewhere but soon found out the Army had other plans for her. Six weeks after John was assigned to Camp Campbell he asked for time to get his wife moved nearby.

His commanding officer's answer was simple, "This is the Army, Lieutenant, you don't get time off unless it's an emergency."

As always before her dad saw to getting her and her things moved to Kentucky but let John take it from there. Belinda's dad had provided the best of everything for his family and she soon realized she had lived a sheltered life. John's meager salary as a Second Lieutenant might not afford them a house off base, but Belinda never imagined living on base and sometimes wondered if it had been a mistake marrying John. Occasionally she even wondered if he was the same man she fell in love with and married.

"Strange as it may sound," John's voice broke into her thoughts. "I have been thinking about the very same thing,"

Belinda was so relieved to know she and John still lived in the same world. "Can we all go for a walk John?" "Can we go right now and look at the houses near us; just to think about what kind of house we want?"

John saw the pleading in her eyes and would have done anything to please his beautiful wife; she didn't have to plead with him. Still, after almost five years of marriage, Belinda was the most beautiful, the most captivating, the most...,

"Of course we can go;" and caught both of his girls by the hand. The rest of the evening was spent looking at houses that *weren't* for sale, or rent. But Belinda felt better just knowing John was willing to make a move for her.

The next two Saturdays John rented a horse and buggy to go looking thru the small towns near Camp Campbell; they settled on Pembroke, in Christian County. A nice house at the edge of town was empty, and for sale. She was so excited to get moved in but the owner wanted five hundred dollars.

"Oh, John, Belinda gasped, five hundred dollars!" "How can we ever pay that much for a house on your salary?"

"I don't know but how can we go wrong living in Christian county?" John stated matter of factly. "Somehow God will provide."

"It will be our home no matter where the Army sends me. I won't have to worry about my girls being safe and or having friends while I'm away from home."

And during the next thirteen years his assumption *seemed* to be so. But very few things in life are *ever* as they appear or *ever* remain unchanged.

****

A year later, after the move to Pembroke, the time for school had come faster than Belinda wanted it to. But, she reasoned, that was probably so with most mothers of their first child. Bettie was six years old *already* and going to school this year. Belinda thought she would walk the short distance with Bettie to Pembroke Elementary School. Other kids were on their way and Belinda knew Bettie could have gone alone but they lived at the edge of town and this was her *first* day. And after all, she was a *mother.*

John was now Captain John Latimer, US Army, and stationed at Camp Campbell a few miles south of Pembroke. They chose Pembroke because it was a small town away from the influence of the Army base or any large city. There was a school and church nearby and the people were friendly. They felt safe letting Bettie have the freedom to run and play without worry of where or what she was doing.

****

During the first morning Mrs. Pepperdine assigned everyone a seat according to their class. With some exceptions but generally from the youngest in front to the oldest in the back. When everyone was settled and had books for all their classes it was eleven thirty. Mrs. Pepperdine told everyone it was lunch time and to put all their books in their desks.

Bettie didn't even know she had a lunch but Mrs. Pepperdine showed her where her mama had left it. When Bettie went running outside with Sadie, her new friend, to find a place to eat their lunch Mrs. Pepperdine smiled thinking how a child's emotions could run from the lowest low to a new high, all in one morning.

The school year had started off with a good morning and even though Mrs. Pepperdine knew there would be problems she was thankful for a good new beginning. *New Beginnings,* she mused, and thought about new beginnings with God. There had been a new beginning with each of God's days of creation, then when Adam and Eve ate the forbidden fruit and were told to leave the garden.

And again after the flood that killed all earthly life except Noah's family and the animals on the Ark. Abraham, Isaac, Jacob, King David, Solomon and of Christ Jesus, all had new beginnings.

Of America, already one hundred and twenty five years old, and all the new inventions, a horseless carriage and plans to make a flying machine. Homes with electricity and telephones; so many new beginnings. So much to teach her students she felt inadequate of the task.

And to limit her student's studies to the few text books in her classroom was like holding a hungry child away from the dinner table when it is loaded with all their favorite food. She would do what she could with what she had and that was all anyone could expect.

She had five first graders experiencing a new beginning of school and sent up a quick prayer for each of them. Bettie Latimer, Sadie Plummer, Billy Johnson, Clarence Clearwater and Johnny Rivers.

When new names came before her she couldn't help wondering about their origin and what had brought them together. She and her husband, Emmet Pepperdine, had both emigrated from England just five years old. She thought Clearwater and Rivers had a Native American sound possibly of the Cherokee or Choctaw people. Johnson was a Swedish name, she knew lots of the Swedish people settled in Iowa and Minnesota. Plummer and Latimer, she wasn't sure but thought probably English or possibly German. All brought together here in the Pembroke Elementary School for her to teach.

Mrs. Pepperdine saw all the kids were settled to eat their lunch then returned to her desk and took out her own lunch, a sandwich of homemade bread with a slice of ham; and then smiled as she set an apple on her desk.

She wondered which of the new students would be first to bring their teacher an apple and guessed it would either be Sadie or Bettie. The boys usually weren't as quick as the girls to make up with their teacher; but each year was different.

She looked at the wind-up clock on her desk and saw it was nearly time to call the kids in from playing. But just as she started for the door she heard a young girl's *scream*. Either "Bettie or Sadie," she thought and hurried to look out. It was neither of the girls she expected to see being tormented by one of the boys with a bug or worm.

But all three of the young boys were thrashing about while the others watched. Billy Johnson was the object of Clarence and Johnny's attention on the ground. Billy was the biggest of the three and held off Clarence until Johnny lit into him.

During their playtime that day Billy made his first attempt to get Bettie's attention by showing off in front of her. Then when she paid him no mind he tried to use force and took hold of her wrist; attempting to pull her into a game. That was the *first time* she would feel his hard grip on her arm.

It was then that her friendship started with Johnny and Clarence. They didn't care for Billy's pushy ways and immediately Clarence attacked Billy and then Johnny jumped in to help his friend fight the bully off her.

Down to the ground the three boys went, arms and legs wrapped around each other; hitting, biting, and rubbing noses to the ground.

From that day forward, all thru school, Bettie, Johnny, and Clarence were inseparable friends.

"Stop that, stop it I say," Mrs. Pepperdine called out to them. "The rest of you kids go inside right now." Two older boys pulled Johnny and Clarence up off the ground as they passed by; Billy was a little slower getting up all the time dusting the dirt off his clothes.

She hurried down the steps to where the three boys stood, now covered with dirt and a few bruises.

"What do you boys mean, fighting like this?" She demanded an answer in her more adult/teacher sounding voice.

"Why were you three fighting? Tell me right now or I will send for all your mothers and let them take you home to tan your britches."

All the older kids knew this wasn't just an *idle* threat Mrs. Pepperdine held over her classroom. It had happened more than once but usually one time a year was all it took to let everyone know she made good on the threat. She wasn't a large lady, actually rather petite, standing just over five feet tall. She would have been no match for any of the older boys. Anyway, by the time they were in the seventh or eighth grade they knew if their dad had to be called in from their work they wouldn't be able to sit for a few days.

Clarence spoke first; "I started it Mrs. Pepperdine, cause Billy was picking on Bettie."

"No, I started it," Johnny offered to take the blame as if he wanted to be first to *confess, or take credit.* Inwardly she wondered *why*. Why would two first grade boys want to take credit for starting a fight at school over the defense of a girl they hadn't known before today?

"Very well, both of you claim to have started it but what I want to know is *why*... Billy, why were you picking on Bettie? Did she bother you first?"

"No," Billy gave a *sullen* answer, he didn't want to answer but knew he better. His dad was a traveling salesman and rarely home but he was home to see Billy start school. He didn't want a licking from his dad before he left home again.

"I'm still waiting Billy, why did you pick on Bettie? Don't you know it isn't nice for boys to pick on girls? Hasn't your dad told you that?"

"My dad would just *laugh* at you if you sent for him and told him he was to whip my britches for picking on a girl."

"He picks on my mama all the time. He says women were *made* for men to enjoy."

She knew at six years of age Billy didn't fully understand what his dad's words meant. But not to be outdone Mrs. Pepperdine took Billy by the arm.

"Your dad might laugh about abusing girls and ladies but I don't," she said. "So I'm not sending for your father, I'll take care of this myself."

"Johnny and Clarence, dust yourselves off, go inside and take your seats we'll be right there."

Mrs. Pepperdine, with Billy by the arm, went around the side of the schoolhouse where she kept her secret paddling board. In no less than two minutes later they entered the schoolhouse with Mrs. Pepperdine still holding to Billy's arm. Billy held his other hand on the seat of his britches. In the same forceful manner she had taken Billy around the schoolhouse she walked him to his seat and, with a little help, said, "Sit down."

With Billy seated she walked to her own desk and sat down. All eyes were on Mrs. Pepperdine now, especially those in the first and second grade who sat wide eyed not expecting to see this side of Mrs. Pepperdine; on the first day of school. She sat for a moment with eyes closed. When she opened her eyes she stood, her smile back in place.

"Now, children where were we?"

They didn't know she had just said a prayer for herself as well as all the kids to have a good year at school. For God's Holy Spirit to have control of all their lives while inside or outside of the classroom.

They didn't understand that spanking Billy Johnson had upset her just as much, if not more, than Billy. She hated having to spank a child, especially on the very first day of school, but

sometimes, it seemed, there was no better way to get a child's attention.
So she did.

Chapter Two

It would soon be one o'clock and Mrs. Pepperdine had to hurry to make assignments for the next day. Her head was throbbing already on the first day of school and all she wanted was for it to be over. Quickly she went around the room going from class to class seeing that each student had the correct books and gave all but the first graders reading assignments. She told them she would have a special science lesson for them the next day and had no assignment.

Back at her desk she turned to face her class. "As you older kids know," she said. And somehow even Bettie knew something different was going to happen. "The first week of school I always take you to see the horses, but today we won't be going."

"You are all dismissed, except Billy Johnson." She told him to stay seated while all the other kids left the room. When everyone was gone outside she said, "I'm going home with you Billy, to speak to your father."

She didn't look forward to a parent confrontation on the very *first* day of school but she thought it best to meet this attitude head on.

She walked beside Billy all the way home and didn't let him go running in ahead of her. From what he had said to her about his dad's estimation of women she didn't want to give him the advantage. She held on to Billy's arm while she knocked on the door. The sound of a man's voice, and from his words she was sure it was Billy's dad, could be heard inside.

"*Woman,* there's someone at the door."

"I'm going Henry," a ladies pleasant sounding voice answered in return.

"That's Mama," Billy said and looked nervous for the first time.

The door opened but before Irma Johnson could speak Mrs. Pepperdine introduced herself as Billy's school teacher.

"We had a bit of trouble today and I thought it best to get it settled with you and Mr. Johnson. I understand he is home."

She knew from Billy, and from hearing his voice he was home, but spoke to Mrs. Johnson in such a way Mrs. Johnson understood she knew he was there and wanted to speak to him as well.

"Billy, did you cause your teacher trouble the very first day of school?" Mrs. Johnson asked.

Again Mrs. Pepperdine was quick to keep Billy quiet. "I'm here to speak to you and Billy's father," she said authoritatively. If what Billy told her about his dad's appraisal of women was correct, she wanted to keep ahead of any intimidation directed at her.

She didn't *ask* if she might speak to him as though she needed *his* permission to speak. She had handled problems with parents before and found that sometimes she needed to assert herself; especially with men. She didn't look for problems but when one jumped out at her she wasn't one to back down; and this, she felt, was one of those times.

"Of course, he is right inside, please come in."

Irma Johnson was the typical small town housewife of the day, not dowdy nor modern, just common. She wore an everyday faded down, pale yellow dress. Her hands revealed she worked her garden and flower beds as well as whatever else she could do to keep the house up. From what Billy had said about his dad being a traveling salesman Mrs. Pepperdine doubted that he ever did anything to help her with the house.

"Who is it," he *growled* out the question. Irritation sounding in his voice that anyone would be bothering him at home.

"It's Billy's school teacher. She said Billy caused some trouble today and wants to talk to you."

Mrs. Pepperdine was ready for Mr. Johnson's belittlement of the situation of Billy's abusive behavior. Before he could speak she extended her right hand.

"Mr. Johnson, it's so nice to meet you, I've been hearing so many nice things about you."

"Lier, lier pants are on fire," she thought.

She hadn't heard one single nice thing about Henry Johnson but she was *buttering him up for the kill*, as some would say. She continued without giving him a chance to speak.

"I believe though, you are giving Billy the misconception that women are expendable, unimportant, pieces of men's property. To be taken, used and then discarded at their pleasure."

"Billy spoke to me, this very morning, in a most disrespectable tone and I will not tolerate it from him, from you, or any other man."

"And another thing, I used my board on the seat of his britches and I will do it again if this attitude continues."

"Do I make myself clear?" Mr. Johnson.

Henry Johnson stood with his mouth slightly agap not being allowed to speak until Mrs. Pepperdine was thru. He didn't intentionally do so but found himself *nodding* that he understood.

With Henry's nod of understanding Mrs. Pepperdine felt she had accomplished her goal of asserting womanhood and took her leave feeling quite satisfied that she had handled the situation.

She had taken the *bull by the horns*, as her dad used to say. Feeling her mission was accomplished she returned to the school.

After her departure Billy looked up. "Dad, why did you let her talk to you like that?"

"She ain't nobody but a bossy woman."

Henry Johnson's face was red now with anger. Never before had he let a woman talk to him like this, no one except his *mother,* and that was a long time ago. He always hated it when his mama called him down or spanked his behind. Even then he thought it not right for a woman, his mother or any other woman, to spank a boy. One day after cussing his mother she slapped his face and then stuck a bar of soap in his mouth.

Well, Henry Johnson hadn't changed his attitude toward women. Now, instead of his mother it was his wife who received the brunt of his ill behavior. And not only that, but Billy was learning to behave just like him. When he was home his time spent with Billy was telling him about what a great life he led, doing what he wanted to do without having a woman boss him around. Most of the time Henry was happy to see his son take after him but today wouldn't be one of those times.

Right now his pride was hurt, having a woman talk to him like that in his own house was uncalled for.

"It was humiliating to have Mrs. Pepperdine come in here and talk to me like she did, right in front of you and your mother."

Suddenly he seemed to realize who the cause of all this humiliation belonged to. "And Billy, he said, you are the cause of it all."

"Billy, haven't I always told you to stand up for yourself? Well, this better never happen again or I'll show you what a man's licking is like."

"Billy, I came home just to see you get started to school, and now I reckon you have. You watch your step and mind your p's and q's. I'll be gone tomorrow before you get home from school."

Henry's routine was to be gone for three or four weeks at a time and then one evening show up as if he hadn't been gone but the day. He'd carry an old suitcase full of dirty shirts that Irma washed and ironed, get his suit cleaned up, his shoes shined and after a couple days he'd be off again. Like he couldn't sit still in one place. He always told Irma it was the only kind of work he ever wanted to do and she needn't try to hold him back.

Irma never understood what she might be holding Henry Johnson back from. He had always been a wanderer, even when he and Irma first married Henry only stayed home a few days. When she asked if he didn't want to stay with his new wife his response had been, *"Other people* are depending on me too, I can't just stay in Pembroke."

She always wondered though who the other people were that depended on him when he never had but a few dollars to give her. If her folks hadn't left her their house she didn't know how she would make ends meet for her and Billy. She couldn't help but wonder if having a house was the only reason Henry had married her.

****

When Mrs. Pepperdine left the Johnson's house she was *shaking* so badly she could hardly walk back to the schoolhouse. Her legs felt like jelly, her heart was beating like a show horse, and she even felt a little faint.

"What have I done," she chided herself.

In all my years of teaching I've never had anything so *infuriate* me as Billy Johnson's attitude. Maybe I overreacted, maybe I shouldn't have spanked Billy, and maybe I shouldn't have spoken to Mr. Johnson as I did. I will certainly have to pray for Billy and myself not to let this happen again.

Starting right then as she sat in the quiet of the schoolhouse she prayed not only for Billy, but Johnny, Clarence, Bettie, Sadie and all the others. Twenty nine students this year, the highest number of kids she had ever had at Pembroke Elementary School. She was so glad to have the first day over and going home; hoping it would ease her headache. She would have supper ready when her husband Emmet came in for the evening.

After fifteen years of marriage she still longed to hear his voice say, *"Claudia, I'm home."* She had longed for children of her own and figured teaching was God's way of giving her both sons and daughters to look after. Most days she enjoyed her time at school, just being around young people helped fill her yearning for children of her own. She had prayed and asked God to give her and Emmet a child but it didn't happen.

She had prayed, "Lord, let me have a child of my own and I'll be the best mother ever." She cried, wailed, begged, all to no avail. Finally, she had to give in to being a stand-in mother as a teacher.

"How was your first day at school? Do you have very many new kids this year?" He always showed an interest in her life. That was the reason she had married him, that and the fact she loved him more than anyone else in the world.

"I'll tell you about it after supper," she smiled back and gave him a kiss on the cheek.

He raised an eyebrow, "Already you are giving me a kiss and we haven't eaten supper, you must have had an exceptionally good day or an awfully bad one."

"Emmet, come sit down I've fixed you creamed peas and potatoes along with a thick slice of ham. We have pecan pie for dessert."

After they ate their supper and the dishes were cleaned up she went to sit by Emmet in their rocking chairs. He hadn't prodded his wife any further about her day knowing it would come when she was ready.

Her mother said she was born ten days late and had never caught up. Right away Emmet learned that everything was done in her time.

"I *spanked* a boy today, she said, and I'm not sure if I was more insulted by him or by what his father has been teaching him."

"Emmet, do you know Henry and Irma Johnson?" Without waiting for his answer she went on as he knew she would and didn't try to answer Claudia until she had her say.

"Their son Billy started school today and caused trouble on the playground the very first day of school."

"I walked him home after I let school out and gave his father a piece of my mind."

Emmet smiled and reached for her hand, "You want to be careful about who you give pieces of your mind to, some day you might find you need it back."

His teasing made her feel better, she was thankful for that. Thankful for him. And for the Lord Jesus who she knew would keep her heart, and soul, and *mind* safe for always.

Chapter Three

None of the other kids knew what took place at Billy's house and he wasn't about to tell anyone. He didn't want anyone to know that Mrs. Pepperdine had visited his parent's house or the way she talked to his dad. The next day when she rang the bell all twenty nine students came inside without a word; still a little *stunned* from her actions the day before. Truth be told, so was she.

When recess time came she took a folding chair and sat at the open door, just to see for herself if anything happened. Billy, Johnny and Clarence had all seemed fine with each other when they came inside that morning. Yesterday might be a forgotten memory to three six year old boys, she hoped so. As a teacher she wanted to share her love equally with all three boys. But for some reason there was a nagging, foreboding feeling in her heart that wouldn't let go.

All the kids went running out to play, for some, recess was the best part of school. At home all the kids weren't nearby and couldn't play together like they did at school. The younger girls liked to skip rope or play hop scotch, while the older girls might join in or just sit and talk. The younger boys would play tag, run races or pester the older boys into letting them join into whatever they were doing.

At first Mrs. Pepperdine thought everyone was in the groups she expected but then she noticed Johnny, Clarence and Bettie had pulled away from the others. They weren't really doing anything but sitting together, watching the others and this puzzled her. It was more than unusual for three young children, not all boys or all girls, to form a bond this quick. She wondered if it had anything to do with yesterday's incident.

She looked for Billy, was he playing or was he planning to get even somehow. Even though he was playing tag with the other boys she wasn't sure but thought she saw him watching them. Then when he went tearing in front of the three and smiled at Bettie she knew it wasn't over. Could this all be a case of *young jealousy,* could Billy just be trying to get Bettie's attention in the only way he knew how? She could only hope it would pass with time.

All the rest of the week school was out at one o'clock and Mrs. Pepperdine led all the kids to the horse barn to see the show horses. Bettie didn't know what a show horse was but a man Mrs.

Pepperdine knew told them all about each of the horses. Bettie even touched one's nose, or it touched her, she wasn't sure. Johnny stood on one side of her and Clarence on the other; just to make sure nothing happened to her.

All that first school year Mrs. Pepperdine kept her eye on those three young students hoping to see them take Sadie and Billy into their circle of close friendship. If Billy had a good friend that was a *girl* it might help him to see his dad's opinion of women was wrong. However, that didn't happen, Johnny, Clarence, and Bettie could always be found together. No matter how much she encouraged them to join in with the other kid's games they could always be found doing something else, together.

****

It was an unusual relationship, two boys and one girl. She didn't think Bettie lived near either of the boys so they hadn't been together before school, why did she only want to be with them here? It almost seemed like they were protecting her. Did they still think Billy might harm Bettie if they weren't near her? She could only shake her head puzzled at the situation.

Mrs. Pepperdine didn't know that starting their very first day of school Johnny and Clarence walked Bettie home from school. Belinda was on the front porch waiting and watching for Bettie that first day. She almost walked back to the school house for Bettie but decided to let her be on her own and go with the others to see the horses.

She was almost as bad as Bettie had been that morning not wanting her to go and would have stayed if Mrs. Pepperdine had asked her to. As she waited she was surprised to see Bettie along with two boys, one walking on either side of her when they neared the house.

The boys walked along beside Bettie like little tin soldiers. She smiled at them and wondered how Bettie had made friends with them so soon. When they saw Belinda waiting the boys suddenly stopped and went in another direction.

Belinda took Bettie by the hand and gave me a hug. "Who are your friends?"

Bettie looked at her mama as if not understanding the question.

"The two boys you were walking home with;" Belinda pointed in their direction.

"Oh, that was just Johnny and Clarence."

"Did Johnny and Clarence start school today too?" Bettie simply answered "Yes" before jumping onto a different subject. "Mama, did you know that tadpoles turn into frogs?"

Belinda smiled, "Is that what Mrs. Pepperdine told you today?"

"Oh, no, that's what Johnny and Clarence were talking about coming home. They asked me if I would like to go with them down to the creek sometime and look for tadpoles."

"And what did you tell the boys?"

"I said I probably could next Saturday but I'd have to see if you needed me."

"You can tell them I expect I could get along ok by myself for a while next Saturday."

After watching for Bettie each day that first week and seeing the two boys walking on either side of her, Belinda decided that come Saturday she would invite them in and get to know Bettie's new friends that seemed so.. *protective*.

****

Saturday morning when Johnny and Clarence came walking up to the Latimer house Bettie was sitting on the top porch step waiting.

"Hi," she said with a small wave of her hand.

"Are you two ready to go to the creek?"

She had on one of her old dresses but wished she had a pair of overalls when she saw they were both in their usual overalls only without a shirt today.

Belinda came out just then with a plate of oatmeal cookies still warm from the oven.

"Bettie, ask your friends to come sit on the step with you and have a cookie."

When they seemed reluctant to approach the house, and Belinda, Bettie said, "Come on you guys and set down, don't act like a *scaredy cat*."

Lackadaisically the boys sat on a step below Bettie and waited for her mother's cookies.

"I'm Bettie's mother, Mrs. Latimer. Do you boys have a name?"

"Yes, Mama," Bettie answered for them. "This is Johnny and this is Clarence." She pointed to each one as she spoke.

"Does Johnny and Clarence have a last name?" Belinda asked.

"Yes, Mama, Bettie said again. Johnny is Johnny Rivers and Clarence is Clarence Clearwater."

"Well, Johnny Rivers and Clarence Clearwater, I am glad to finally meet you."

Belinda held out the plate of cookies to each one who looked for the biggest one to take. When they had gobbled down their first cookie Belinda held out the plate for them to take a second one.

"So Johnny Rivers and Clarence Clearwater, I understand you are taking Bettie to the creek to look for tadpoles; is that right?"

They both nodded yes, still without saying a word.

"I see you boys are both big talkers," Belinda teased. She smiled and they both felt a little embarrassed but smiled back without a word.

When they were all ready to go, Bettie said, "Come on you guys," and took off running. Belinda called after them, "Be home in time for supper."

****

It was a hot September that year, but the beginning of school always seemed hot at Pembroke, Kentucky and sometimes rainy. This Saturday morning was no exception, it was a warm day to play along Silver Creek. None of the three had thought about taking their clothes off or wearing shorts to play in the water. Johnny and Clarence just rolled their pant legs up to their knees. Bettie's dress was short enough and they were all bare foot to step in the water. But after an hour of walking up and down the creek bank trying to find a tadpole they were hot and itchy from the weeds.

"I wish we could jump in the swimming hole and cool off," Johnny said.

Clarence's "Yeah, me too," was all it took for Bettie to start jerking her dress up over her head.

"The last one in is a rotten egg," she said.

"Be careful, there is a deep hole up there." Johnny and Clarence both cautioned her but when they saw her still undressing they did too and were right behind her jumping into the water. They all ran the shallow water until they found the deep hole with enough water to jump into. It was cool and felt good to their young sweaty bodies. They dunked each other and played until worn out. When she left the swimming hole and started running down the shallow creek water Johnny and Clarence ran behind her.

They hadn't ever had a girl playmate before and didn't know what to expect, they were going along with whatever she wanted to do. After all boys are young gentlemen in the making; and they were trying.

After running back and forth in the shallow water and taking another turn in the swimming hole they were cooled off and climbed out. Without a towel to dry off with they were wet getting dressed again but they didn't care; a few hours in the hot sun would take care of that. The boys didn't say anything about Bettie being a girl, they were just friends having a good time.

There hadn't been any kids at Camp Campbell for Bettie to play with so Johnny and Clarence were the first real friends she ever had. It didn't bother her being a girl and them boys, they were just friends.

They never did find any tadpoles. All to soon the day slipped by. After tiring of looking for tadpoles, and then taking a dip in the water, the three wandered around from one of their houses to the next. That was the day she found out where Johnny and Clarence lived. In the future she often ran to their houses when she wanted to talk.

As the boys walked her back to her house for the last time that day Clarence said, "Next Saturday let's look for the eagle's nest; Dad said it's down Silver Creek somewhere."

"Why is it called Silver Creek?" Bettie asked.

Clarence was first to answer. "Dad says when his grandpa was young he and two friends saw some men pretending to be Indians, bury a keg of silver coins some place along the creek bank. So ever since then it has always been called Silver Creek."

"Do you think we might find the keg of silver coins?" she asked.

"Naw, we'd never find it," Johnny answered. "Lots of people have looked for it, and we'd never find something buried that long ago."

Bettie looked at him not believing they couldn't find it if they really wanted to. But the beginning of making plans for the next Saturday started and almost every week they all knew *exactly* what their plans were for the next Saturday; and it didn't include anyone but Johnny, Clarence and Bettie.

Chapter Four

Belinda took one look at Bettie and knew she had been in the water. Her hair still showed tangled signs of being wet. Her dress suggested it had been wet too and was now dust covered.

"Young lady have you been in the water?" "From the looks of you no one would know, or even *guess*, that you are a Latimer."

"Oh, Mama, we wanted to jump in the water to cool off and we didn't want to get our clothes wet."

"Anyway, no one else was there and saw us."

"You *undressed* in front of those boys! Bettie Latimer, don't you have any sense of decency, or shame? What do you think your father would say if he knew, and the *neighbors*?"

"Oh, Mama," was all she could think of to say. "It was just Johnny and Clarence, they are my friends."

"And what if you were twenty years old, would you still think it was ok to undress in front of your friends, Johnny and Clarence?"

"Ladies don't undress with men. Ladies are ladies and men are men. It's the way God made us."

"We don't stop being a lady and become a man just because we feel like it."

"Oh, Mama, you know I wouldn't do that."

"Well, *young lady*, see that you don't ever do it again, *not now, not ever*."

"Come on inside and get a bath and some clean clothes; you look like a *waif*."

She didn't know what a waif was but decided not to find out right then and do as her mama said. On the way inside she changed the subject and asked,

"Mama, did you bake any cookies today, I'm starved."

****

Every day at school was the same for the first graders, Billy challenged Johnny or Clarence at every opportunity. You might have thought they were from a tribe of *primal* people just waiting for the opportunity to club the other over the head instead of first grade boys in the twentieth century.

Mrs. Pepperdine watched them every day just to make sure there were no more fights. But, still it was amusing to her to watch Johnny,

Clarence and Billy sparring around each other. Such young boys to be so interested in one girl.

Something Mrs. Pepperdine didn't know was that one day Billy attempted to walk home with Bettie alone. He tried to get rid of the other two and have her alone but that only drew the three of them closer. Billy was bigger than either Johnny or Clarence but together they sent Billy running for home. After that there was hardly ever a time that all three of them weren't together. And that was just the beginning of school.

****

"Where are you kids going to play today?" Belinda asked Bettie knowing that Johnny and Clarence would no doubt be showing up any time. Bettie was helping her mama clean up after breakfast.

"Clarence said there is an eagle's nest some place down Silver Creek, we are going to look for it today."

"Oh, Mama wouldn't it be the most wonderful thing to see a real live eagle? Mrs. Pepperdine talked about eagles one day and showed us pictures. If we find it do you think there might be baby eagles in the nest?"

"I don't know Bettie," and Belinda smiled to herself. "I don't know any Eagles *personally* so I don't know when they have their babies."

"Oh, Mama you are being silly."

Just then she looked toward the door and saw Johnny and Clarence in their bib overalls and no shirt, standing on the porch.

"Come on in you guys," She called to them. "I'll be ready in a minute."

"Mama, she *whispered,* can I take my dress off and wear overalls like they do?"

Belinda felt her little girl slipping away from her each time Bettie pushed at the boundary for young ladies. When she was a little girl her daddy would have *raged* like a bear had any of his girls dressed in pants. But times were changing, she had even heard talk about women having the right to *vote*; the same as men. She didn't know how John felt about that but secretly thought she would feel good about getting to vote.

"All right, Belinda sighed, go upstairs and change into some pants that I made you for winter. They are folded up in your dresser drawer."

"Now, boys," Belinda asked. "How long is this *expedition* going to take? I suppose you plan on being home in time for supper."

"But what about dinner, don't you ever get hungry at noon unless you are told to come in and eat?"

They looked at each other as if no-one had ever posed that question to them before. When they both shrugged their shoulders without answering Belinda asked, "You do know English don't you?"

"So far I haven't heard either of you two boys say a word."

After saying it Belinda wished she could take it back, it just slipped out intended to sound like a joke. But what if they didn't know English or what if there was a reason they couldn't talk and she had shamed them? She would feel terrible and regret it the rest of her life. Suddenly she placed her hand over her mouth.

"Oh, I'm sorry, she gasped, I wasn't making fun of you boys."

Johnny looked at Clarence, they both folded their arms across their chest and nodded, "*Ugg*, we speak English plenty good. We know... many words."

Johnny spoke slowly as if he was having to think of each word and translate it into English. Neither boy spoke or cracked a smile as they stood *stoically* waiting for Bettie to return. They could have been their Great, Great, Grandfathers of the Cherokee or Choctaw Nations who had once occupied this part of Kentucky.

Just then Bettie came bouncing down the stairs wearing only her bib overalls and a big smile all ready to go; feeling like one of the boys. Belinda gasped at sight of her remembering the boys were there.

"Bettie Latimer, she said, you get yourself back upstairs and put your shirt on."

"Boy do you look different," Johnny declared forgetting his pretense of native Indian background.

"If you didn't have long hair I couldn't tell you from Clarence."

"Why you boys have been putting me on with your old way of talking," Belinda laughed.

"Ugg, me fix you all lunch sack so brave warriors won't get hungry before you return. Expedition might be *loooong*." Without smiling Belinda raised her right hand and indicated an imaginary long line.

Just then Bettie came back down the stairs with a shirt on and saw her mama stretch out her arm.

"What did you say?"

"Johnny, Clarence and I have heap big secret."

"I, pale faced woman, fix lunch now."

Soon they were off and running, with Johnny and Clarence laughing about how Belinda had caught on to their joke and pretended along with them.

They went to the creek and found a place they could cross to the other side without getting wet. Clarence took the lead.

"My dad said it's at least two miles down the creek where he saw an eagle and thought it must have a nest close by."

"Do you think there might be any baby eagles in the nest?" Bettie asked.

Clarence was leading, Bettie was next with Johnny behind. It was always like that with them however they walked, whether in line or side by side, Bettie was in the middle with Johnny and Clarence on either side.

They were silent for a while, if three six year olds can be silent. Anyway, Clarence was leading the way and Bettie was trying to keep up, this was her first real expedition, as her mama had put it. Only one time she asked Clarence, "Are we about there? How far is two miles? I don't know if I can walk that far?"

He stopped and looked at Bettie with such a scorching look that his eyes said,

"Don't be a complaining girl." After that she didn't ask again.

When they came to a place that was clear of weeds Clarence held up his hand.

"We'll rest here."

"Johnny, we need to have pow wow with Bettie, she needs an Indian name like ours. Got any ideas?"

"How about Bettie Rivers?"

"How about Bettie Clearwater?" Clarence retorted.

"How about Bettie Clearriver? Johnny came back.

"How about Bettie Creekwater?" Clarence said.

"How about Bettie Silvercreek?" Bettie jumped in. "After all it is my name, and I like Silvercreek."

"Ok, by me Johnny if that's what Bettie likes."

Johnny agreed. "From now on, and for ever more, she will be known as Bettie Silvercreek. Let's make an Indian promise to always be friends with Bettie Silvercreek."

Johnny held out his hand and spit in it. Clarence did the same and waited for Bettie. When she hesitated Clarence said, "Go on, if you want-a-be Bettie Silvercreek and be a real Indian, spit in your hand and then put it with ours. We'll make a real Indian pledge."

It wasn't that she didn't want to become a real Indian she just wasn't sure what her mama would think about her changing her name. After running the pros and cons thru her mind their came a *hucck* from her throat and then she spit in her hand. After that they all placed their spit on hands together.

"From this day on," Clarence said placing a final seal to their friendship. *"Bettie Silvercreek, Johnny Rivers and Clarence Clearwater will be eternally bound to help and protect each other."*

None of the three had any idea what lay in their future or what being eternally bound together would mean, even in their physical lives. But such is the mind of six year old kids, the first twenty years of a kid's life seems like an eternity. And being forty years old made one appear super ancient, so eternal to them could mean anything over forty.

"That was good Clarence, Johnny complimented his friend. Did you read that someplace?"

"Naw, just made it up."

"We need to go on now, you guys ready?" He asked.

They all stood and fell into line again just as before. The braves protecting the squaw and no one ever knew of the *pact* that sealed their friendship or why they wouldn't be separated.

They all walked silent as Indians each with their own young thoughts not knowing the extent of the pact they had just made to help and protect each other. If only they could have looked just twelve years into that eternal pact they made they would have seen a different future than any of them imagined.

None of these three brave Indians knew what an eagle's nest looked like so they really didn't know what they were looking for. But Bettie Silvercreek spotted a large bunch of leaves that looked like a nest, up in the top of a tree and thought she had found it.

"Look," she whispered and pointed. "Is that an eagles nest?"

"I dunno, Johnny whispered back. Let's all throw a rock at it and see if we can scare out whatever is in the nest."

After several unsuccessful attempts at hitting the nest, their rocks falling far short, Clarence said,

"Lets climb the tree," but also found the tree was too big to climb.

"Let's climb a smaller tree that we *can* climb and then maybe we can throw a rock high enough to hit it," Bettie suggested.

The boys thought it worth a try and gave her a boost up to get started, then they followed. She had never climbed trees before and found it to be so much fun she actually forgot about finding the eagle's nest. When they were exhausted from climbing and throwing rocks they decided to rest and eat the lunch Belinda had sent with them.

"Ugg, sandwiches plenty good," Bettie said. The boys nodded their agreement. After their rest Clarence suggested,

"Let's go back home and stop by the creek, we can look for the nest another day."

After a morning of walking in weeds, climbing trees and throwing rocks they all had the same thing on their minds. By the time they came back to the swimming hole they couldn't resist. At first Bettie remembered her mama saying, "Bettie Latimer, promise me you won't do that again."

But then Bettie remembered with Johnny and Clarence, she wasn't Bettie Latimer any more but *Bettie Silvercreek,* and thought it would be ok.

"Last one in is a rotten egg," she called.

Off went their clothes and they were soon enjoying the cool water. Bettie felt pretty certain her mama would never know.

Chapter Five

The rest of August and September soon slipped by without the Indian blood brothers and sister trio finding the eagle's nest. After a couple of Saturdays of throwing rocks at s*quirrels nests,* and them not knowing the difference, seeing an eagle's nest lost some of its interest.

"We'll watch for the eagles, and next year, Clarence conceded, we'll find it for sure."

With the coming of October the swimming hole was losing its appeal since the weather had become noticeably cooler. One Saturday morning the two boys came to the Latimer house and plopped down on the bottom porch step to wait for Bettie. They didn't knock on the door, holler, or know yet to, just go on inside. Instead, they sat down to wait for her to come outside. After sitting in the warm sunshine for several minutes they became drowsy and were soon taking a nap.

Since the cooler night temperature had made the house cool Belinda still had the door closed and Bettie couldn't see the boys waiting on the step.

Since they were sitting on the bottom step with their heads down they weren't visible to her when she did look for them. The early morning wore on and she was anxiously waiting for them to show up and get started doing something, anything but stay in the house.

"Where could Johnny and Clarence be?" she asked after every trip to look outside.

"They are probably like Little Boy Blue, behind the haystack fast asleep," her mama teased her.

"Oh, Mama, don't be silly. You know there aren't any haystacks around here."

"Mr. Teague has a haystack," Belinda reminded her. "They could be asleep there."

When she didn't go running off to find out if they were behind Mr. Teague's haystack Belinda said;

"Why don't *you* go find them for once?"

"Ok, Mama, I will."

That was all the encouragement she needed and bound for the door. She closed both doors behind her and headed for the steps going down; all ready for a run. Without looking for, or expecting, anyone on the steps she tripped over Johnny and Clarence and went flying right over their head to land with a nasty *plop* on the hard ground. She landed on her back that knocked the air out of her body.

"Ohoo," she gasped.

Johnny and Clarence, awake now from their slumber, jumped up. "Bettie, are you hurt?" "Bettie are you ok?" "Bettie are you…"

She held up her hand, a signal to stop with the questions. It took her a minute to regain her senses and breathe enough to sit up.

"Yes, I'm ok. What happened?"

"We've been waiting for you on the steps."

"We thought you'd never come out today," Clarence sounded a wee bit peeved.

"Well, I've been waiting for you inside, all morning." Bettie countered.

Belinda had heard the noise and went to the door just in time to hear the exchange. It was the first time she had heard an irritated word from either of them and she wondered if it meant anything. Some kids can be the best of friends one day and the worst enemy the next. She wondered what she would hear next. They had been *true-blue, tighter than glue* friends since school started, maybe this was a testing ground but she didn't understand what she heard next.

"Come on Bettie Silvercreek," Johnny said. "We'll *help* you up." And both boys took hold of her hands to pull her to her feet. She brushed her pants off, "Would you guys like to eat a fresh cookie with me?" She asked and they all started up the steps. "*Unbelievable*," Belinda thought.

"Hi boys," Belinda called to them as if she hadn't witnessed the scene outside. "Did you sleep late this morning?"

"No, Mama," Bettie answered for them.

"They were sitting on the porch steps all morning while I waited for them inside. But we are going to have a cookie before we go any place."

"All right, dear." "Do you boys ever help your mother bake cookies like Bettie helps me?"

"Naw," Bettie answered for them again. Belinda noticed Bettie had picked up one of the boy's words.

"Their mothers don't want a boy helping them make cookies."

"Bettie, do you always answer for Johnny and Clarence at school?"

"Not always but sometimes," Bettie seemed not to notice her mother's insinuation.

Belinda folded her arms across her chest and took a stance that would have *rivaled* the most fearless of Indian Chiefs.

"Ugg, smart Indian braves learn how to make cookies for self, maybe pale faced woman not always make for you."

First Clarence and then Johnny folded their arms as Belinda had and masked their face with the most unyielding expression they could muster up.

"Ugg, Clarence replied, me understand."

"Pale face woman speak with straight tongue."

"Ugg, Johnny also said, me believe pale faced woman speak true words."

Bettie missed the boy's first exchange of Indian talk with her mama so she didn't catch on until after Johnny had spoken. Then she also matched their stance with the most stoic expression she could manage.

"Ugg," she said. "I, Bettie Silvercreek, also believe pale faced woman speak true words."

Belinda continued to play their game while remembering as a young girl she had seen real Indians when her dad had taken his family out of town for a buggy ride. While the family rode in their plush seated buggy, all dressed in nice clothes, she remembered the Indian kids ragged clothes and hungry faces. She remembered them because she was a kid herself and felt sorry for them. After seeing their poor faces standing along the road she had never wanted to play cowboy and Indian games with her younger brother and sister.

"Come on you three Indians, and I'll give you your first cookie baking lesson. But first all of you make a trip to the privy and then we will all wash our hands with soap and water."

"You boys do know what soap is, don't you?"

Belinda smiled at the youngsters and then shooed them outside toward the privy. "Don't take all day or pale faced woman will change her mind."

Minutes later they all came running back inside and once again Belinda pointed them toward the wash basin. "Everyone use soap," she reminded them.

"Bettie, while I build up the fire in the stove to get it hot again, show the boys where everything is. See if you remember everything we need to make cookies and place it on the table."

Belinda came back with three aprons and helped each of the Indian braves into one. "Ugg," she said. "Don't worry these won't make braves look like pale faced woman."

"Ugg," they all replied with faces a little pinker than usual.

Belinda showed them how to mix the flour, eggs, milk, lard, and baking powder. After the oats were added she allowed each one of her helpers to take a turn at working them into the flour. The boys were delighted to help, they laughed and giggled like girls. The kitchen would have been a bigger mess than it already was if she hadn't been there to supervise.

"Ok," she said. "Now let's make some cookies," and showed them how to take a spoonful of dough, then drop it on to the cookie sheet a couple or so inches apart.

When the cookie sheet was full of an odd assortment of cookie dough she placed it in the oven. While the boys waited to taste their very first, ever baked cookie Belinda helped them get cleaned up and took their aprons off. The kitchen was beginning to smell of fresh baked cookies and the boys were more anxious about getting them out than Bettie was.

When they were baked Belinda took the hot pan out of the oven and slid the cookies off onto a towel to cool.

There wasn't any doubt when she asked,

"Do you three think you could drink a glass of milk and eat some fresh baked cookie now?"

The boys didn't seem to notice the cookies they had made were odd sized or *peculiar* duplications of the one Belinda made.

Chapter Six

Summer 1906

When John, that is Major Latimer to his Army friends at Camp Campbell, had his weekend pass once a month he always planned to come home. But since he and Belinda felt a car wasn't in their tight budget, he rode home on the train. Belinda told Bettie they couldn't afford a car.

"They are too expensive," she had told Bettie.

"A new car could cost as much as a $1,000.00." So her daddy had to ride the train twenty five miles up from Camp Campbell to Pembroke. He wrote Belinda every month and told her when or if he would have a weekend pass so they could watch for him.

John was supposed to be on his way home that morning and Bettie sat waiting, anxious to run throw my arms around him and tell him she loved him and how happy she was to see him. She was going to have her *own* daddy home for a change and was watching for some sign of his arrival.

It was the last weekend of May, sunny and warm that Saturday morning. She didn't know much about the Army then but her daddy told her other soldiers were to call him Major Latimer instead of saying, "Hi John, how you doing today."

"That's just the *Army Way*," he told her more than once. "We don't ask why we just do things the Army way and everyone is happier that way." He would smile then so she supposed he must be happy being in the Army.

As usual, she expected to see him come walking from the train station in Pembroke toward their house and was sitting on the front porch steps waiting. But this time as she waited her daddy didn't come walking up the road. Instead she saw a *motor car*. She had never seen a motor car before but it was coming toward their house and she wondered who it could be.

No one in Pembroke owned a motor car. She had heard the talk of Mr. Hanks at the General Store and Mr. Edwards who was both a lawyer and judge, wanting to order one. But as of yet neither of them had one. She had scarcely even seen a picture of one until that morning.

The driver brought it to a stop in front of their house and then pulled eye coverings up from his face.

"Daddy, she *squealed*. "You are driving a motor car."

She ran to climb in beside him. "Where did you get it?" She asked and a thousand other things too fast for him to answer. Her daddy just sat there and listened. Then he pushed a black button in the middle of the wheel he steered with that caused it to make the funniest noise.

"*Ooga, ooga, ooga,*" it went.

She laughed at the sound and about that time Belinda came rushing from the front door.

She put her hand to her head "What on earth?"

"John, where on earth did you get that *contraption*?"

"It isn't a contraption, Belinda, it's a *motor car*."

"Come on and get in, be the first lady in Pembroke to ride in an Adams-Farwell 1905 motor car, from Dubuque, Iowa."

He pushed the black button again and it made that funny noise. "*Ooga, ooga, ooga,*" it said to Belinda.

Belinda climbed into the seat and pulled Bettie back onto her lap. John climbed out and went to the front end where an iron rod bent in the shape of the letter Z stuck out. He gave the rod a pull and turn that started the motor car running again. "*Chuckle chuckle, chuckle chuckle,*" it said. Then it would do it again, "*Chuckle chuckle, chuckle chuckle.*"

"Hold on." John said. Then he pulled the funny looking things back down over his eyes. He pushed a lever forward and the motor car began to move. Bettie squealed with laughter again and clapped her hands.

"Go *faster* Daddy, go faster," she cried.

"No, John, don't go faster," Belinda cried just as fast. "We don't want to have a wreck going this fast."

John drove up and down Pembroke's main street a couple of times just to make sure Mr. Hanks and Mr. Edwards both saw them. He waved his hand at no one in particular when we passed the General Store. He didn't care if they saw him but he wanted to make sure everyone saw Belinda riding in a motor car. He truly loved her and would do anything to prove it.

"Drive by Johnny and Clarence's house," Bettie said. "I want them to ride in a motor car too."

"*Ooga, ooga, ooga,*" her daddy made the motor car make that funny noise in front of Clarence's house. Clarence came running outside to see the funny noise maker and stopped with his mouth open. George and Maude were right behind him and all three stood for a moment taking in the sight.

"Come on folks," John called to them. "Lets all take a ride."

After they were all seated John once again pushed the lever forward and the motor car began it's, "*Chuckle chuckle, chuckle chuckle,*" as we started toward Johnny's house.

John made the motor car make that funny *"Ooga, ooga, ooga."* Bettie thought it so funny she laughed every time and this time Clarence laughed too. Her daddy pulled the lever back and brought it to a stop in front of Johnny's house where he, William and Minnie all poured out of the house to see the contraption; as Belinda had called it.

"Johnny," Bettie hollered. "Come on and get in." But it wasn't just Johnny that wanted to take a ride in the motor car.

"What about Minnie and I," William asked.

"Don't we get to take a ride too?"

John waved to them and called for them to get in the back seat with George and Maude. That was going to make nine people in the motor car. But four adults could hardly get seated in the back seat and finally George said, "Wait, I've got an idea," and climbed out of the back seat.

"I'll stand on the running board on one side and William, you stand on the other running board. The ladies and kids can sit in the seat."

By now it wasn't just Johnny's family wanting to see the motor car; men and boys had followed them along the way from Clarence's house until they stopped. Now there were a crowd of people around the motor car; including some neighborhood ladies. They all crowded around the motor car wanting to have a closer look. One elderly man, a Mr. Stevens, at first stood at the edge of the crowd. He had come to Kentucky back when there wasn't another *white* man within fifty miles. Maybe more, maybe a hundred.

Old man Stevens reached a bony finger toward the motor car and lightly touched it.

"My eyes have seed everthin now, *everthin* there is to see."

He said it and turned away as if that was the last new thing he would ever see. His words were reminiscent of the old man's words at the temple when Mary and Joseph brought baby Jesus to be dedicated to the Lord. He said, "Mine eyes have see the *glory* of the Lord, now I can die in peace." The next day old man Steven's was found lying in his bed; already gone on to meet his maker.

John made the motor car go, "*Ooga, ooga, ooga,*" again trying to get everyone's attention to move the motor car. Then William and George took their caps off and waved them around shouting like they were boys riding a wild bull. It wasn't until the second time John made the motor car go, "*Ooga, ooga, ooga,*" and moved the lever forward a bit causing it to start moving that the people moved out of the way.

They all waved and their friends *waved* back at them as if they were going away on a trip. The motor car started making its usual, "Chuckle *chuckle, chuckle chuckle, chuckle chuckle chuckle,*" and they were off down the road toward Hopkinsville. There was a cross roads along the way called, Casky, where John turned the car around and went back to Pembroke.

They went back by the River's and Clearwater's houses to let the parents out and the crowd of people was still standing around talking.

George and William pumped their legs up and down on the running boards and hollered while waving their caps. Once again they were young boys riding a wild bull. As the motor car slowed down they turned loose and jumped to the ground to help Maude and Minnie out of the back seat.

"Can Johnny and Clarence ride home with us," Bettie asked her mama hoping Johnny's mama and Clarence's mama would hear her and say, "Ok."

"They may if its ok with their parents," Belinda said. Right then Belinda was so happy she would have agreed to anything Bettie asked her for. She couldn't stop smiling in spite of the fact she had been *scared stiff* when John made the motor car go fast. There was a round thing with glass on its front and numbers inside starting with 0, and then 10, 20, 30, 40, 50.

More than once Bettie saw her give her daddy a concerned look when the needle pointed at 40 mph. She didn't know what, mph meant except the motor car went faster the higher the number the needle pointed at.

"Yes, they may ride along," Maude and Minnie both said. "But send them back home when you want to be rid of them," Maude went on.

"They can be as sticky as a fly catcher," Minnie said and laughed about their boys.

John made the motor car go, "*Ooga, ooga, ooga,*" and everyone moved back out of way for the motor car to pass.

Belinda's legs were shaky when John helped her out of the motor car, she brushed her hair back and smoothed her dress.

"My legs feel as weak as a kitten." "Thanks, she said, for making me the first lady in Pembroke to ride in a motor car, but you haven't bought this contraption, *have you*?"

"And where in the world is Dubuque, Iowa?"

Belinda took Bettie's hand as if she were a small child and walked them both into the house. John just sat there in the Adams-Farwell motor car along with Johnny and Clarence. For once neither of her friends seemed the least bit interested in what she was doing. Bettie saw them both running their hands over the leather seat with a look that said, "Hope my dad gets one of these."

John spent the next hour showing Johnny and Clarence how to start the motor and then shut it off. How you could steer it with just that one little wheel he sat behind. They even got to *sit* in the seat and make the "Ooga, ooga, ooga" noise

After an hour of looking all three *"boys"* came trudging into the house.

Chapter Seven

Summer 1906

    Bettie was always happy to see her daddy, but especially that weekend. They rode in the motor car two more times before John had to go back to Camp Campbell. She grew up knowing that he couldn't be home all the time like regular dads. Johnny and Clarence's dads worked most of the year at Gray Gate's Strawberry Farm two miles south of town. They would have walked to work every morning and back home every evening except for an old *black* man named Moses. Now, Moses drove his old mule and wagon into town every morning, just to pick up all the men.
    They were always gone to work before Bettie was up to see them but she had heard about Moses singing as he drove his old mule along the road. She had heard enough talk of it that she wanted to hear for herself.

"Mama, may I ride in the wagon with Johnny and Clarence and their daddy's to work?"

"I want to hear the old black man sing his songs. Can I Mama?"

Belinda's first answer was what Bettie expected it would be, "No Bettie, you are seven years old and have no business riding in a wagon full of men."

She waited a couple of days before asking again. This time she reminded her mama that Johnny and Clarence's daddy's rode in the wagon. And if Johnny and Clarence were with her she wouldn't be alone. And, they could all walk back home together.

"Pleaseee, Mama," she begged. "I want to hear the old black man sing."

This time she added what she hoped would be the clincher. "The old man sings spiritual songs about Jesus."

When Belinda didn't give her a quick 'no' as before she knew she was half way there. She didn't think Maude or Minnie would object to having the boys ride in the wagon so with that bit of progress she gave her mama an extra big hug with, "Thanks Mama, I love you."

Belinda saw right thru her little prank; she didn't fool her for a minute. Belinda waited two whole days before walking with Bettie to town and then suggesting they stop and see Maude Clearwater and Minnie Rivers. Bettie felt all a quiver inside but didn't tell her mama.

"I need to run to the outhouse first," she said.

Bettie walked to town with Belinda being ever so careful not to say anything that would upset her. When Belinda was thru in the General Store she said, "Ok, you little *conniver,* come on with me and we'll go talk to Maude and Minnie."

The next morning they were on the wagon with William, George and a dozen other men from town. They had worked at the strawberry farm five years and couldn't remember a day old Moses not singing while he drove them to work. When Moses pulled his old mule to a stop that morning he looked puzzled at seeing three youngsters.

"These be new slaves fo Mr. Gray?" He cackled a laugh then started singing. *"Get on board lil chillun, get on board lil chillun, get on board lil chillun, Dere's room for many-a-more.*

"I hear de train a comin, I hears her close at hand, I hear de car wheels rumblin, And rolling through de land."

"Get on board lil chillun, get on board lil children, get on board lil children, Dere's room for many-a-more."

"Da fare is cheap, And all can go, da rich and poor are der, No second class upon dis train, No difference in de fare."

"Get on board lil chillun, get on board lil chillun, get on board lil chillun, Dere's room for many-a-more."

****

Bettie could see his hands barely moving trying to clap to the rhythm of his song.

"What be your name, lil Missy," Moses asked.

"My friends, Johnny and Clarence here, call me Bettie Silvercreek," she said.

"Can you sing, Bettie Silbercreek?"

"Oh, no, Mr. Moses," she answered quickly.

"I don't sing. But I'd like to hear you sing us another song." And without missing a beat Moses began to sing in a deeper voice.

"Go Down Moses," and they all understood why he would sing, *"Go down Moses, Way down in Egypt land, Tell ole Pharaoh, To let My people go."*

"When Israel was in Egypt land, Let My people go, Oppressed so hard the' could not stand, Let My people go."

"Thus spoke the Lawd," bold Moses said, *"If not, I'll smite your first born dead, Let My people go."*

As soon as he finished that song he started on another one.

"Climbin Up Da Mountain, chillun, Didn't come here to stay. And if I nevermore see you again, Gonna meet you at de judgement day."

"Hebrew in da fiery furnace, And dey begin to pray, And da good Lawd smote dat fire out, Oh wasn't dat a mighty day! Good Lawd, wasn't dat a mighty day!"

"Daniel went in da lions den, And he begin to pray, And da angels of da Lawd locked da lion's jaw, Good Lawd, wasn't dat a mighty day!"

George Clearwater couldn't help asking Moses why he always sang, what he had so much to be happy about?

"Well, sa," Ole Moses smiled. "I's has a whole bunch of things to be *happy* bout, da fust is dat *I sings causin I know's the Lawd and He knows me.* Dat makes me happy all o'va, and thru and thru."

"Da second thing is, when I's was a young man my masta had *a white man drive me* to wurk eva day with a long whip."

"Now, me an ole Ginny dere, pointing to his mule, *we drives white men* to wurk eva day while we gos and sits in da shade."

"About noon time I asks for a glass of lemonade and Ole Ginny gets her a drink of cool wata, den we sits in da shade some moe."

Just then Ole Moses broke out into another song. "I sings ba causin I'm happy, I sings ba causin I'm free. His eye is on da sparrow but I knows He watchs me."

Moses smiled a toothless smile that spread all across his happy face. He gave Ole Ginny a slight jiggle of her rein to let her know she was to keep moving. It wasn't necessary for the men to ever ask again because everyone could see old Moses was a happy man. They *thought* he had worked as a slave for Mr. Gray's daddy but now young Mr. Gray gave him a place to live out his days in peace. Mr. Gray never asked Moses to drive his wagon into town every morning; he just did. Truth be known that was another one of the reasons why Moses was so happy every morning; he could still get up and be with the men.

Along the way William Rivers said to Moses, "Moses, do you have a last name?"

"Well sa," and Ole Moses thought on it a bit. "Iff'in I has a last name I reckon it would be Gray."

"Yes sa, I reckon my name would be Gray."
"I likes the sound of that, Moses Gray." "Umm humm, I'd be a Gray then and not jus another Ole black man." He cackled his little laugh at the thought.

"I reckon Mista Gray done gib me everthing I has so's I reckon he wouldn't mind gibin me his name."

"Ole Mista Gray he pay fifty dollars for me when I was young, strong, an good lookin."

"Then you know what Mista Gray do fo Moses, he takes me to his home an *pays me* to wurk fo him."

Moses laughed a funny little cackle of wonder.

"How old are you Moses?" The question was asked that took Moses a while to ponder the answer.

"Well sa," Moses replied starting his backwards way of remembering; because he really didn't know for sure when he was born or how old he was.

"I remembers Mista Abraham Lincoln setting the slaves free; that was in 18 and 63. I was already a free slave by Mista Gray but Mista Lincoln say all the slaves ought to be free."

"Then I remembers Mista Andrew Jackson causin Mista Gray buy me from Mista Jackson before he is President. In 18 and 38 Mista President Jackson send all the Cherokee Indians west to Indian territory but I didn't have to move like the Indians, I had a home right here with Mista Gray."

"Then I remembers on the 4th of July, 18 and 26. Nobody wurked on the 4th of July, but that year I's be rememberin causin Mista Tomas Jefferson and Mista John Adams both die that day."

"Then I remembers the War of 1812, that was the year Mista Gray buy me from Mista Jackson afta Mista Jackson bring 26 slaves from Natchez to Nashville and sell um."

"So, you were born around Natchez, Mississippi?" George asked.

"I reckons so, but don't rightly know."

Moses went on. "I's was jus a young boy then so's I reckon I be born about 1800."

"Moses, that would make you be at least 107 years old," William said for him in amazement.

"Umm humm, I reckon I be that," Moses gave a nod. "Moses, how many of our Presidents can you remember?" William asked not expecting Moses to name but a few.

"Well sa," Moses scratched his head in thought. "I reckon I remembers jus about all of umm ceptin Washington, Adams, an Jefferson."

"Yes sa, I remembers Madison, Monroe, John Q. Adams, Jackson, Van Buren, and Harrison, he died jus a month afta being President."

"Then come Tyler, Polk, Taylor, Fillmore, Pierce, Buchanan, Abe Lincoln, an Johnson, who never attended school. Maybe I be President someday like Mista Johnson." Moses cackled his little laugh.

"Then there was Grant, Hayes, and Garfield that got his self shot."

"Afta Garfield come Arthur, Cleveland, Harrison, and Cleveland again. Then McKinley, an now we gots Teddy Roosevelt."

The men all listened to Moses in amazement never thinking he had any education. None of the men listening could have named all the Presidents; in order as Moses just had.

Then Moses began to sing his song and they were all bond by it's words.

"We've come a long way, Lawd, a mighty long way. We've borne our burdens in the heat of the day. But we know the Lawd has made the way, We've come a long way, Lawd, a mighty long way."

"I've been in the valley and prayed night and day, And I know the Lawd has made the way.

I've hard trials each and ev'ry day
But I know the Lawd has made the way."

"Wish I was in Heb'en sitting down,
Wish I was in Heb'en sitting down.
O, Mary, O, Martha,
Wish I was in Heb'en sitting down."

"Wouldn't get tired no more, tired no more,
Wouldn't have nothing to do, nothing to do."

"Try on my long white robe, long white robe
An sit at my Jesus feet, my Jesus feet."

Moses finished his song just as Ginny pulled the wagon up by the barn where the men jumped out.

"Thanks for singing us some of your songs, Mr. Moses," Bettie said along with Johnny and Clarence.

"You's mighty welcom, missy."

Then just before they jumped from his wagon old Moses asked them the strangest question they'd ever heard. "Missy, Johnny, Clarence, does you youngens know the Lawd and does He know you?"

"It be mighty important that you do."

They didn't know how to answer Moses' question so they all jumped out of the back end of his wagon and started back home. Moses was the only black man she had ever talked to but he talked using the same words white people did so she guessed it didn't matter what color you were. Just then Clarence said;

"Missy, does you know the Lawd?" Johnny finished what Moses asked, "And does He know you?"

She started to sing and clap her hands together just as she imagined old Moses would have done even though his hands hardly moved. Johnny and Clarence picked up right behind her and all the way home they clapped their hands along with Bettie and sang;

"Get on board lil chillun, get on board lil chillun, Dere's room for many-a- more.

They repeated old Moses song several times not understanding the significance of the words, "to get on board."

She wondered what Moses had meant when he asked if they knew the Lawd and if the Lawd knew them.

"Johnny, do you know?" she asked.

When he shook his head and said, "I dunno," she asked Clarence. When Clarence said, "I dunno either," she determined to find out somehow.

Chapter Eight

Summer 1907

Their second school year had passed, they were eight years old now, and it was a Saturday summer morning. Like most small town kids they were always looking for something different to do. Most days they played up and down the banks of Silver Creek part of the day. But one day when all three of their minds seemed to be at a blank for activity Belinda gave them an idea and then wished she hadn't.

"You three should be forest rangers. You could stand on a lookout tower high in the hills and watch out for forest fires."

She always wondered where in the world that idea came from and why she would share it with three *roaming* kids. She didn't even know there was a lookout tower the kids could walk to but after she saw Johnny and Clarence's eyes light up she knew she had made a mistake.

"Hey, that's a good idea," Clarence almost shouted. "There's a lookout tower back in the woods, but it's *pretty far* away."

"Its way back up in the hills some place."

"I've heard my dad talk about it too," Johnny said just as excited as Clarence at the idea of finding it.

"Hey, whoa you three." Belinda jumped to thwart the idea before it was too late.

"I was only joking, you kids are not, and I repeat, *are not* going way back in the hills alone."

"I don't care if a fungus grows on your feet sitting here bored to death. And Belinda repeated herself, "You are not to go *alone* looking for a lookout tower way back in the hills. There could be a Black Bear or a Bobcat, or who knows what's up in those hills."

The faces of all three kids were all but dragging the floor when they left the Latimer house. Belinda wasn't sure anymore if she lived in the Latimer house or Silvercreek house but she tried to be the adult.

"I'm an Indian now Mama," Bettie said it over and over. "My Indian name is Bettie Silvercreek."

She had told Belinda, at least fifty times, she was going to find that keg of silver coins. After finding out about the legend of a keg of silver coins being buried somewhere along the creek bank. She was sure they could find it if they would only try hard enough.

"That was at least seventy five years ago." "Maybe a hundred years have passed since then and no one even knows for sure that there ever was a keg of silver coins buried."

Belinda tried to reason with her about such a legend but her talks always ended the same way.

"It might be a legend and it might not be, but if it's there I'll find it."

Bettie was so sure she would find the silver Belinda would drop the subject until the next time. She thought the kids were safe looking for the silver along the creek banks and after a few times didn't watch them any more; it was only a short distance from the house.

And after all the years that had passed since the legend started she didn't expect them to engage anyone else in town interested enough to help them look. But trapesing around way back in the hills and woods alone, "No, not her child."

At least she hoped she had headed that idea off before it took *flight* because she wasn't completely sure she had. Those three eight year old minds were like a train's steam engine; always chugging out more steam, filled with ideas.

They were about to wander off looking for something, anything, when John drove in using a motor car he borrowed from Camp Campbell. Bettie went running to see him.

"Hi daddy," and he bent over for a big hug.

"What are you kids doing today?"

"Oh, nothing," she moaned. "Mama won't let us go looking for a lookout tower back in the hills."

He shook his head sympathetically. "Umm umm umm." "Do you suppose she would let you go if I went with you?"

"Oh, Daddy, would *'you'* ask her?" "I *'love'* you so much Daddy."

"Please Daddy, ask her." "Please."

She jumped into his arms and wrapped her arms around his neck as if she was still a small child; anything but what Belinda had been dealing with every day. She watched her *conniving* little girl from the front porch and remembered how her sister Charlotte had charmed their daddy into doing things he never dreamed of doing. When he let loose of the little *charmer* and looked up Belinda was waiting.

"Ok, what did she talk you into this time?" All fathers are alike, she thought, with a conniving daughter.

"Bettie said something about wanting to go for a walk and find a lookout tower but you wouldn't let her."

"Do you suppose it would be all right if I took her?"

"And would the prettiest lady in the world be interested in going with us on such an expedition?"

"And husbands are all alike too when they want something."

"You know I would, John Latimer, you needn't use your charm on me."

"I'd follow you to the ends of the earth."

John wrapped his arms around Belinda and kissed her soundly right there on the front porch in front of the kids.

After John's unexpected forwardness and Belinda had stopped blushing and regained her composure, John asked;

"What do you boys think about looking for a lookout tower? Are your parents busy today?"

Their faces lit up now seeing the possibilities of doing something besides hanging around the house every day.

"My mom and dad are both home," Clarence was first to answer.

"Mine too," Johnny added. "Maybe we can get them to go too. We'll go see."

And off they ran. It wasn't long before the Rivers and Clearwater families both came walking up the road to find out what the boys were so excited about.

"These boys say you'd like to go find the lookout tower back in the hills, is that right?" George Clearwater called.

"George and I were just boys when the state put that up to look out over the hills," William Rivers continued.

"We always wanted to find a way to get all the way to the top but never did."

"Well, maybe we can find a way, let's go see."

"Wait a minute George, Maude called the men down like she was talking to the boys. It always happened between them two. If one didn't start it the other one would. To the outsider their banter might have sounded like a terrible fight was brewing but it never did so their friends knew it was just their way of getting along. If Maude hadn't already started George would tease her until she did.

"Now, Maude, if we don't get going it will be too late to go today. Tomorrow is Sunday and you don't want to be no back slider and not go to church tomorrow, do you?"

Maude didn't like being called a back slider and was momentarily stilled by her husbands comment.

"William, is there any way to drive this car part way that would get us any closer?" John asked.

"Yes, an old logging road runs back into the hills the Forest Rangers used to haul lumber close to the site. But the ruts might be a little rough for your car."

"We'll see, ladies get your walking shoes on and lets go. Belinda can you fix us a jug of water? I'll change out of my uniform and be ready to go."

"I've got the only walking shoes on that I own," Maude said and Minnie said, "Me too."

"Then I'll be right back," John told them.

Four adults and three kids all piled into John's borrowed car while George and William stood on the running boards. John drove with Bettie and Belinda in the front seat beside him.

Minnie, Maude, Johnny and Clarence were in the back seat.

William and George stood on the running boards giving John directions to the logging road and half an hour later they were to the turn off.

"Now, the fun part starts," John told the others as he turned on to the bumpy road.

"With this many people in the car it could drag over a deep rut and damage the car."

"If it looks too bad John, don't try to drive any farther, we can all walk," Belinda assured him.

"How *far* a walk are we talking about?" Minnie wondered.

"You men are better walkers than us ladies. If it's too far I may have to wait for you to get back."

But she really had no intention of waiting as the others went on to find the tower.

"What if a Black Bear came by?" She said out loud.

"Or a mountain lion.

"Now, Minnie, William soothed her. "Don't get all *hett* up, you might blow a gasket."

The other two men smiled but didn't speak.

She had no sooner spoken the words when John stopped the car.

"See those ruts up ahead, I think we better stop here before I get the car stuck. I can turn around here to go back."

"How much farther do you think it is?" Minnie asked again.

"Another mile or two, maybe more, maybe less," William looked at George for his agreement.

Getting out of the car in the middle of the woods on a logging road was like a dream come true for those kids. They took off running as if they couldn't bear waiting another minute to see the tower.

"Slow down you three Indians," Belinda called after them. "If it's still there it'll stand a *few* more minutes while us older people can get there."

Johnny, Clarence and Bettie were in the middle of the rutted area when George called to her.

"Don't stop, gal, keep going." She didn't know why but didn't stop running until she was past the ruts.

"Look in the rut John, I'll get me a big stick and take care of that Copper Head laying there in the sun."

"See, William," Minnie said nervously to prove her point. "That Copper Head could have bit me and I'd be dead when you come back this way."

"Yeah, but it wouldn't have carried you off like a Black Bear could so keep your eyes open for a bear."

George looked at William in a knowing way but John wasn't privy to their practical joke.

The men helped their wives get passed the deep rutted area, and any more possible snakes, then they fell into two groups of men and women.

They weren't nearly as anxious to see the tower as the kids who ran back and forth in front of their parents. By the time they reached the tower, they could have been there two or three times with all their running back and forth.

"Wow," Belinda heard Bettie say. "Is that ever big?" "I didn't expect it to be so tall."

Then all three kids started in. "Come on, Mom and Dad," "We want to climb the steps and look out."

"Wait up kids," came from all three mothers. It sounded like they had rehearsed what they would say.

"Let your dad make sure it's safe before you climb on it. We don't want any broken arms or legs today."

Then the men heard, "Be careful John." "Be careful William." "Be careful George."

The men all looked at their angst wives as if to say, "Don't worry Mama, we are big boys now."

So far on this outing John had to stop the car, Bettie walked right over a Copper Head, they had walked two miles thru the woods, and now the mothers all said wait up.

But the dads didn't seem nearly as concerned.

"Don't worry about climbing up the tower," they all said to the mothers. "It looks safe."

"I'll stop worrying when everyone's feet are on the ground and we are all walking into church tomorrow with no broken bones," Maude countered.

Belinda and Minnie both nodded their agreement, that the men should be careful.

"There might be rotten boards from this standing out here so many years. You men be careful."

"Yes, dear," John answered. "We will be."

They looked at the steps going up that turned back and forth every twelve steps. The third set of steps ended at the bottom of a platform that held a small room on the very top. The platform appeared to be solid above the steps.

"How do we get up on the platform?"

"That's a good question, John," George and I could never get past that trap door, they put a lock on it to keep kids from getting to the top."

"And dads too," Minnie added. "I hope you men know you aren't supposed to be up there."

"Now Minnie,"...., William started but stopped in mid sentence. He put his finger to his lips, "Shush everyone."

"Don't anyone say anything, he whispered and put a finger to his lips again, everyone move very quietly toward the steps. Kids go first and then you ladies."

"If we don't all make it up the steps, I'll run for help."

The other adults looked at William with questioning stares but no one spoke. No one was laughing now and all the horror stories ever told about people mysteriously disappearing in the Kentucky woods seemed real.

The kids were no longer thinking about climbing on top of the platform. The boys were quiet and Bettie could feel the hair on her arms standing up.

As they all huddled solemnly at the first landing John was able to ask William what it was about.

"Over there," he barely whispered and gave John a *wink*. He nodded his head in a certain direction; "I think I saw a Black Bear."

They all looked but couldn't see the bear. "Are you sure?" George asked. "Are you sure it was a bear?"

"Maybe it was an Indian."

"I'm sure," William said. "Let's give it a few minutes to see if it comes after us; if it doesn't we'll beat it out of here."

Breathlessly they all stood huddled to one another as if the world was about to end, but nothing happened.

After a few minutes had passed and no sign of a bear, William quietly told the rest of them to move to the bottom of the steps.

"You boys take Bettie's hands and, *walk don't run*, in front of us."

"Men take your wife's hand and don't *anyone* talk, be very quiet."

"Just listen to the sounds in the trees. Maybe the bear won't hear us and we'll get back home alive."

The walk back to the car was peaceful and quiet. They could hear Fox Squirrels barking in the trees ahead of them and birds were noticed that hadn't been before. There was no grumbling about walking, the heat or the bear. The jar of water Belinda brought was passed around twice and it was all gone. John turned the car around and everyone piled in as before to ride out of the woods.

Minnie hadn't said another word to the men about being careful or not trying to get on top of the platform. The kids were satisfied that they had been on the tower and the ladies were happy they were all going home with no injuries to take care of.

On the way home George looked over at William with a knowing smile. Since they were kids this had been an old game between them.

Chapter Nine

Summer 1908

When you are nine years old *life* is about as easy and carefree as it ever gets. And that was true for Bettie Latimer Silvercreek, Johnny Rivers and Clarence Clearwater; up until this summer. But that was about to change.

Everything they did was as three Indians. They were so close mouthed around their mamas the ladies hardly knew where they were or what they were doing. Belinda didn't want to ask Bettie any more about the three of them skinny dipping. She knew they did even though she had told Bettie not to.

Belinda thought Bettie was contrary to everything she told her. As sure as Belinda told her not to do something, that's just what she wanted to do.

As the hot summer days passed they were always looking for something *new* to do; something different. But anything new was hard to come across and the yearning to find the keg of silver coins was always on Bettie's mind; if not Johnny and Clarence's.

The keg of silver coins wasn't a new story to the boys but she had never heard about it until a couple of years ago; and now she couldn't stop thinking about it."

"One day, she told herself, I'm going to find that keg and have all the silver that's been waiting for me to find."

No one *she* had talked to hardly paid her any mind about it and knew she'd never find something buried a hundred years ago. But there was one old man in Pembroke, only known as, "Whispering Pete," *she* hadn't talked to. At the General Store, Mr. Hanks told her that years and years, and *years* ago, Whispering Pete was known as Pembroke Pete. But when he got so old he could hardly talk his name was changed to Whispering Pete.

"You might try talking to him, if you can still hear him whisper," Mr. Hanks told Bettie.

She'd try, she told Mr. Hanks, and the three of them headed off in the direction of Whispering Pete's house.

Whispering Pete's house was a two roomed house that looked as old as Pete. It was the only log cabin she had ever seen anyone living in and appeared to be near ready to collapse. Before moving to Pembroke Bettie's family had lived in a small house on base at Camp Campbell, but it had *three* rooms. As she looked at his little house she reckoned two rooms was enough for one old man.

Whispering Pete's house set way at the northeast edge of town; overlooking a stretch of Silver Creek. No one else lived near his house so they hadn't had reason to go there before that day.

She was told Whispering Pete sat on his front porch all day without talking to anyone. He only had one chair and he sat on it, so he didn't invite anyone to sit and talk with him. She thought Whispering Pete's face looked like a dried up prune and he must be at least a hundred years old; maybe older. All of his teeth had fallen out and his gray hair hung shoulder length; cut straight across the top of his shoulders.

She thought he looked more like an old woman than a man but scary as he was Bettie had determined to talk to Whispering Pete. Johnny and Clarence had advised against it but this was one thing she had to do whether *they* wanted to or not.

"We don't even want to get near Whispering Pete," Clarence had said more than once.

Johnny added that his dad told him Whispering Pete had taken more than one white man's scalp when he was a young man.

"You mean Whispering Pete is a *real* Indian?" She was even more sure now that she had to talk to him.

"Mr. Hanks said his name was changed to Whispering Pete because he could hardly talk out loud."

"Maybe he used to whisper but I've never even heard him make a sound," Johnny said.

"I dunno if he can talk any more."

After that she wondered if he *could* even talk but knew she had to try.

"Clarence, did you ever hear him say anything?" she asked.

"Not me," Clarence was quick to say.

"I never wanted to get close enough to him that he could grab me. I don't want to be scalped."

"Me neither," Johnny said.

"Well, if you've never talked to him how do you know he *can't* talk?

She gave both Johnny and Clarence a disgusted look that set both of them in the place of a gnat. To be so young she had the knack for setting both boys straight and they never, or usually never, argued with her. This being one of those times she led Johnny and Clarence right up to Whispering Pete's front porch where he sat.

"Hi Whispering Pete," she said. "I want to talk to you."

Whispering Pete never blinked an eye, didn't change the direction he was staring, didn't say hello or in any other way acknowledge her. She looked at Johnny and Clarence to make sure they were still with her.

"Maybe he can't *hear* or *speak*," Johnny said.

So she moved over in front of his line of vision and waved her arms while jumping up and down. Still nothing happened.

"I wonder if he can't *see*, either," Clarence questioned.

Bettie was ready to go up to him and touch his shoulder but Johnny and Clarence both grabbed her and shook their heads no.

"Don't get near him, he might scalp you," Johnny whispered to her.

They both held on to her like she was getting ready to jump to her death. She shook loose from their hands and stepped up on his porch. She was just about to lay her hand on his shoulder and say hi to him again when he turned his head and smiled.

"Welcome home, *Running Water*," he said so low it was scarcely more than a rasp.

"*I've* been waiting for you many moons."

"You h have?" she stammered. "What for?"

"Run Bettie," Clarence and Johnny both hollered. "He's going to scalp you."

For some reason she couldn't move, she felt like her shoes were nailed to the floor. She remained by Whispering Pete's side and waited for him to speak again knowing she had to be near him to hear.

"Come on Bettie, Johnny urged, while you can still get away."

Whispering Pete hadn't moved again, it seemed turning his head had taken all the energy he had left. Bettie wondered if his body was almost run down and how long it would be before he could move again; so she stayed close by.

She looked into his sunken eyes that seemed to be boring a hole thru her and couldn't keep from asking again why he was waiting for *her,* and how long had he been waiting.

"Why did you call me Running Water? My name is Bettie Silvercreek, and why have you been waiting for me?" she asked again.

Still, Whispering Pete hadn't moved a *twitch* but she felt glued to his side until he gave her an answer. It had been so long since he last talked she guessed he had to get his mouth and tongue working again.

"Come on Bettie, Johnny urged, while you still have your hair." "You don't want him to hang it up beside the other scalps he's taken, do you?"

"Good grief Johnny, you and Clarence be quiet." She glowered. "I'm trying to talk to Whispering Pete."

It seemed that Whispering Pete had to rebuild his strength to explain and whispered; "I watch over Silver Creek and wait many moons for Running Water Silvercreek to come back to me."

"I was young man when I see *white* men dressed like *Choctaw* braves bury keg of silver along creek bank."

"I, young *Cherokee* brave, know white men not Choctaw braves. I, *Eagle Eye*, with friends *Falling Rock and Flying Eagle*, take keg of silver from their hiding place and keep for Running Water. I start calling her Running Water Silvercreek then and promise to build nice house and marry her. But in 1838 President Jackson ordered all Cherokee Indians be sent west to Indian territory."

"I not want to leave my home and hide."

"Running Water go with family but I hide from soldiers with friends, Falling Rock and Flying Eagle. They help Eagle Eye build house for Running Water."

"Long time I wait for Running Water Silvercreek to come back to me."

"Eagle Eye know white men robbers all live near Pembroke and never tell I have keg of silver."

"Every night I watch white men named Johnson, Hanks, Walker, Whitfield, Fletcher, Oats, Gamblin, and Wyatt look along creek bank for the keg of silver they steal but not find.

"If they found the keg of silver, white men plan to say they see Indians bury along creek bank, but they never find silver."

"When they couldn't find the keg of silver each man began to think one of the others had come back alone and taken the silver."

"The men drank fire water, the one named Whitfield bragged he saw Indians bury a keg of silver coins along the creek bank. Our creek became known as Silver Creek then even though no silver was ever found." Pete's face revealed the faintest smile, a slight glimmer was in his eyes.

"All the time they look I have silver coins hid for Running Water to return some day."

"Many moons I wait and think maybe I die before she come back to me. But when I hear Bettie Silvercreek's name whispered from the trees I know Running Water has come back to me."

"This is nice house I build for Running Water. Keg of silver is by her bed, waiting for her to come home."

"I lay on floor and watch for her all night, not sleep in marriage bed alone."

He stopped talking/whispering just as suddenly as he started; still with that staring look in his eyes. Bettie still wasn't sure that he could actually see her or if he just knew she was there.

"The trees whispered my name to you and you have the keg of silver setting in your house?" she asked.

"You do know I'm too young to get married, don't you Whispering Pete?" "I'm only nine years old."

Bettie asked still wondering if he could see her. She wondered if he had her mixed up with the young girl he had promised to marry some day.

"Whispering Pete, do you mind if I go inside and see the keg of silver? So many people have looked for it and all this time you never told anyone you had it. Johnny and Clarence can stay outside with you."

She waited for his answer until she wondered if he could talk any more after all he'd just said. Finally his mouth opened, "Go." She saw his word more than hear it.

She looked at Johnny and Clarence. "It's a trap, don't go inside;" they both mouthed the words so Pete wouldn't hear.

"He'll scalp you."

Bettie looked at them both and would have called them chicken livered ground puppies but since she was talking to Whispering Pete she didn't want him to think she was talking to him.

From the cabin's shabby outside appearance she expected it to be the same on the inside but she was in for the surprise of her life.

"Gracious," she said to no one in particular and stood with her mouth open in awe of what she saw. Whispering Pete really had built a house for a bride that never saw it. Silver coins lay all over the bed. The keg with the remaining coins set by its side. Everything looked like it had just been made. She crossed the room to touch the silver, if she never saw it again she wanted to make sure that it was real.

"Should I take one as proof?" "No," she thought and slipped back outside before Whispering Pete had time to think she was bothering his things.

"It's beautiful." She said to Whispering Pete.

"Your Running Water Silvercreek surely would have loved living here."

In one of his more lucid moments Whispering Pete looked at her as if seeing her for the first time.

"Last time I see Running Water Silvercreek she wasn't much taller than you."

"Running Water didn't reach Indian territory," Pete explained. "She too weak, she die on trail of tears."

"Some day I walk to Indian territory and see my Running Water's grave."

"Maybe tomorrow I go."

Chapter Ten

When they left Whispering Pete's house all Bettie could think of to say to him was, "See ye Whispering Pete," like he had another hundred years to live.

"I'll come see you again real soon."

They ran from Whispering Pete's house to the creek bank where they often sat and talked. Bettie couldn't wait to tell Johnny and Clarence that she touched the silver coins so many people had looked for. They plopped down breathing hard.

"He has it," was all she could manage to say. She had to wait to get her breath before going on.

"Whispering Pete *has* the keg of silver coins; I *touched* them!" Her face glowed as the shiny silver coins she told about seeing.

"Did you see any scalps hanging on the wall," Johnny asked more interested in scalps than silver; plainly his own scalp.

"We watched Whispering Pete real close when you went inside," Clarence huffed, still breathing hard. "If he had moved we were ready to scream for you to get out."

She gave both of them a shove. "I *saw* the keg of silver coins, didn't you hear me?"

"All bright and shiny as a brand new ten cent piece."

"How big is the keg?" Clarence asked.

"I dunno," she shrugged. "Just a keg."

"Taller than a coal bucket, Johnny asked."

"I dunno, she said again, it's about this tall."

She showed them by putting her hand against her knee."

"After all these years *I* found the keg of silver coins."

She didn't know what to do about it now that the silver had been found, or how to let everyone know. But somehow she wanted to let *everyone* in Pembroke know that she, Bettie Silvercreek, found the keg of silver after no one else could.

Right about then Clarence reminded Bettie that it wasn't really her that found the keg of silver coins. Good for old Clarence keeping her straight by pouring cold water on her thoughts.

"You didn't really *find* the keg, Bettie, he said, it was *never* lost. Whispering Pete has had it all the time."

She looked at him like a sizzling hot iron he had just poured water on. A look that would have melted the silver in his hands had he been holding it.

"Ok, she conceded, it wasn't really lost." "But no one would have ever known he has it if *I* hadn't forced you two to go with me."

"You know what I think," Johnny asked, then continued on talking before Clarence or Bettie had a chance to ask what he was thinking.

"Whispering Pete has kept the keg of silver all these years without telling anyone. I think we should ask him what he wants us to do before we tell anyone."

He spit on his hand and held it out. Clarence did the same and placed it on Johnny's. They both looked at Bettie until she did the same sealing the decision to ask Whispering Pete.

The next day Bettie knew she had to go see Whispering Pete again. All morning she stayed inside with her mama until Johnny and Clarence sauntered up to her house as if there was nothing in the world to do that day. She was watching for them and waiting. Bettie didn't know it but Belinda had noticed her pacing back and forth to the front door looking out for the boys.

"Johnny and Clarence are here Mama, I'm going to go outside now and see what they want to do."

"Ok, Bettie dear, have fun. And be sweet," she added.

For some reason that last part bothered her but she knew what she had to do. She grabbed them both to turn around and follow her and then headed for the creek where they would be alone.

"We've got to go back and see Whispering Pete today. We have to talk to him about the silver before he dies."

"We have to know what he wants done with the silver he has spent his whole life keeping."

Johnny nor Clarence really wanted to go back so soon but when Bettie said that they *had* to go, they tagged along as if they had no other choice.

They walked up to Whispering Pete's log cabin and found him sitting on his chair just the way he had been the day before; sitting, staring at nothing, unmoving. It seemed that he never moved enough to even breathe. They could see he held some of the silver coins in his hand and knew from that he had been up some time.

"Hi Whispering Pete," she said. "It's me Bettie Silvercreek and my friends are Johnny Rivers and Clarence Clearwater. We came to talk to you about the keg of silver coins."

Before Pete spoke he sat motionless for the longest time; as he had the day before. When he turned his head he opened his hand with three silver coins.

"For you," he said. "Johnny's Great Grandpa, *Falling Rock Rivers*, and Clarence's Great Grandpa, *Flying Eagle Clearwater* my friends, they help me carry keg of silver to new hiding place."

"My Cherokee name, Eagle Eye, cause I always see Bluecoat soldiers first. Now, I watch you, Johnny, and Clarence at the creek too."

"Falling Rock and Flying Eagle buy white squaw from white man with many daughters."

"I wait for Running Water."

****

Each time Whispering Pete spoke it seemed to take all of his energy. He had to rest then before going on; to even talk. Bettie had never seen anyone so weak.

When Whispering Pete told them he had been friends with Johnny and Clarence's Great Grandpa's they suddenly weren't afraid any more and moved in close to hear every word he said.

While Bettie waited for him to speak again she looked at the large silver dollars and noticed that on the front of each one was a lady with the word Liberty above her picture and the year 1803, engraved at the bottom. A big eagle was on the back.

Finally he began to talk again.

"White men dressed like braves steal pack mule from Bluecoat soldiers loaded with keg of silver coins, maybe taking to Fort Leavenworth to pay soldiers?"

"I not steal from Bluecoat chief, I steal from white men braves. They not *true* braves, Eagle Eye know difference."

"Whispering Pete," she said. "We have come to ask you what *you* want us to do with the keg of silver coins when you can't keep it any longer."

"Long time, many moons ago, I make map to show where keg is buried when I die but I get too old."

"Need help now to bury silver?"

An old piece of paper lay in his lap he now tried to pick up so Bettie helped him. The crude picture looked like his cabin, the large oak tree standing behind it, and then an 'x' marked at the end of three dashes.

"Silver coins will always look over Silvercreek and wait for Running Water to come home."

"You keep," he said to her.

Bettie handed one of the silver dollars to Johnny and one to Clarence; it was their first time to see them.

"Silver coins worth much money," Whispering Pete whispered.

After his friends, Falling Rock and Flying Eagle died, no one but her, Johnny, and Clarence ever knew Whispering Pete had kept the silver coins all those years.

Whispering Pete sat motionless except for his lips moving. It happened so unexpectedly she didn't move, or even think about moving, when Whispering Pete placed his hand on hers. He looked into her eyes then with a piercing gaze.

"Thank you," he said and she saw a tear about to spill out of his eye. Then he slid his weathered old hand back and turned his head to stare out into nothing.

They worked all afternoon getting a hole dug and the keg of silver slid out to it. Whispering Pete had a deer skin wrapped around the wooden keg to keep out water. Again they buried the keg of silver dollars as it once was buried along Silvercreek.

They walked home uncertain what to do with the map or the silver dollar they each carried. One thing they all knew was that they could never let anyone know they had them.

"Maybe we should bury them, and the map," Bettie said.

When they went home that day all of their mamas wanted to know how they got so dirty and where they had been digging. They all gave the same agreed upon answer, "Looking for the keg of silver *supposed* to have been buried along the creek bank."

They all three agreed it wasn't a complete lie to say they had been looking for the silver or that they had been digging for it.

The following morning Johnny and Clarence came running up to Bettie's house.

"Bettie," Clarence called from the screen door. "Are you ready to go?"

Before answering she glanced at Belinda to see if she could read her thoughts.

"Are you kids up to something you shouldn't be," she asked.

"No Mama, I don't think so. We just went to Whispering Pete's house and talked to him."

"Mama, did you know he is a *real* Indian?"

"And real old too, he must be a hundred years old," She went on blathering trying to cover up her nervous feeling. Bettie did that though when she was nervous. She didn't want to lie to Belinda but if her mama asked any more questions Bettie knew she might.

"Come on in," Belinda called to them.

"And have a fresh oatmeal cookie before you start playing."

Sheepishly Johnny and Clarence walked in, both with hands in their overall pockets wondering if they were going to be questioned again about the last couple of days.

They sat down at the kitchen table with Bettie and Belinda brought a fresh batch of cookies from the oven.

"Bettie tells me that you have talked to an old man called Whispering Pete. Did you boys know him?"

"No, but we sure do now," Johnny answered.

They all three sat at the kitchen table and ate two of Belinda's fresh cookies. None of them talked. Belinda tried to find out what they were up to but her questions were scarcely answered. They slipped quietly off their chairs and left the house.

"Bye Mama," Bettie called. "We are going down to the creek."

Leaving the house they walked quietly in single file but as soon as they were away they took off running, *anxious* to get started doing something. They weren't quite sure what it was yet, but something. They didn't know Belinda stood watching, wondering what they were up to. And for two cents she would have followed them to see.

When they reached the tree by the swimming hole they all three plopped down out of breath. They planned to hide their three silver dollars and map by the tree, but what in.

"We need a jar," Bettie said. "One big enough to get the silver dollars in. A jar won't rust or let water ruin them and the map."

"My mama has jars," Clarence said.

"But we need a lid too," Johnny added.

Clarence stood up. "Let's go by my house, I think I can get a jar from the barrel of jars in the smoke house without mama knowing."

"If she asks just tell her we want to use it to put something in down at the creek," Johnny said.

"She'll think we want to catch minnows or frogs."

When they all went trouping into the Clearwater house Mrs. Clearwater smiled at them

"Hi kids, have a chair at the table. I just made some fresh oatmeal cookies, have yourself a couple."

They all looked at each other and sat down. Maude Clearwater made *extra big* cookies and they didn't know if we could eat two more big cookies just yet.

"Maybe just one for me," Bettie told her.

Johnny and Clarence ate both of the warm, soft cookies then they eased outside again.

"We better not go by my house," Johnny said. "My mama was baking cookies this morning too."

They went outside and played around Clarence's house for a few minutes then Clarence slipped quietly around back into the smoke house and found a quart jar with a lid. Johnny and Bettie continued to make noise in front of the house so Mrs. Clearwater wouldn't hear Clarence. He hid the jar under the front of his bibbed overalls and they all started for the creek again.

"Wait, Bettie said, we don't have a shovel to dig a hole."

"My dad has a spade," Johnny said. "But we can't let my mama see us, she might want us to come in and eat more cookies. You two stay back out of sight while I go get the spade. If mama sees me I'll tell her we need to dig for some worms to go fishing."

Finally they got the silver dollars and map in a jar with a tight lid and buried it by the big tree overlooking their swimming hole.

"I think we should go by Whispering Pete's house and tell him everything is all buried and safe," Bettie told the boys.

Only the three of them knew where the silver dollars were buried and Bettie thought Whispering Pete would like to know. Johnny and Clarence both agreed and they were soon standing in front of Whispering Pete's log cabin. But Whispering Pete wasn't sitting on his chair. It seemed *eerily* quiet.

Bettie started to go up on the porch but Johnny and Clarence both grabbed her arms.

"Don't go," Clarence said. "It feels spooky without him sitting there."

"Yeah, he might have put a spell on the house so no one would bother it," Johnny whispered.

Just then Bettie saw a piece of paper lying on his chair and knew it was for her. Shaking their hands loose she said, "Look, he left a note."

It was barely legible, written with the stub of a pencil by Pete's shaky old hand. She had to get the paper and see why Pete wasn't sitting like he had for the last one hundred years. She didn't really know how long he had been sitting there watching, waiting for Running Water but she knew it had been 'many moons,' as Pete put it.
The note read;
Bettie Silvercreek
I leave you my cabin, I go to meet Running Water Silvercreek and join her in Happy Hunting Ground.
Eagle Eye.

Being nine years old she wasn't sure what all that meant but somehow she knew she'd never see Whispering Pete again.

Bettie couldn't imagine the love Whispering Pete must have felt for Running Water, knowing she would never return, yet waiting all these years as if she would.

Chapter Eleven

Fall 1908

Each fall when the kids returned to school Mrs. Pepperdine could see they had all grown but Billy remained the biggest and toughest of the three boys in his class. Each year he challenged Johnny and Clarence to a wrestling match knowing he was the biggest and could best either of them.

"I'll rub your nose in the dirt," he'd boast.

Mrs. Pepperdine heard his boast and watched him to head off any first day of school problems. She didn't want to attempt paddling Billy's britches again and knew it was useless threatening to send for Billy's father; he'd probably just laugh at her.

She noticed Billy and Jack Henderson were friends now even though Jack was a year ahead of Billy. Since Billy was bigger than the other boys his age he and Jack were near the same size. Even though Billy was the youngest of the two it seemed to Mrs. Pepperdine that Billy led Jack around like he was the oldest. She couldn't help but wonder where that kind of friendship would lead to and wondered if it didn't have something to do with Billy's relationship with Johnny and Clarence.

She knew Billy wanted to make them afraid, afraid he would catch one of them alone and carry out his threat. This could be reason enough for Billy's friendship with Jack. She didn't know for sure but thought that was the reason why Johnny and Clarence were always together. They didn't want their nose rubbed against the hard dirt and knew Billy could do it.

By the forth grade Johnny, Clarence and Bettie still showed no desire to join in with the other kids, they were an exclusive club of three. It wasn't the boy's friendship that bothered Mrs. Pepperdine as much as Bettie not having other friends. They were just kids but in three years had shown no interest in anyone but themselves. She felt this wasn't a good relationship to continue and decided to visit each of the three families. Maybe there was a solution and she was missing it.

George and Maude Clearwater were the first parents on her list to visit and had sent a note home with Clarence telling them of her desired meeting. She waited for her Emmet to get home from work and have supper then asked him to go along to meet George Clearwater. She had told Clarence it was a friendly visit and not to be worried about her coming, hoping it would be that. They had all talked briefly at school events but still Clarence thought having your school teacher come to your house was a little scary. He didn't know of another kid Mrs. Pepperdine had visited at home. He couldn't help having that nervous feeling that settles down deep inside a fourth grade boy's stomach.

Emmet and Claudia arrived at the Clearwater's house promptly at seven o'clock and found they were anxiously waiting. It was an informal meeting, no one took down notes of the meeting but the air was a little tense. Mrs. Pepperdine had requested that Clarence stay with them and it was causing him to squirm. Emmet noticed but said nothing, this was Claudia's visit, knowing his wife would get to the matter when she was ready.

Without missing a beat Mrs. Pepperdine said to Clarence;

"I've noticed that you, Johnny and Bettie are always together but no one else ever joins you, why is that? Why don't you play with the other kids at school?"

Clarence turned a little pink being suddenly put in the spotlight. He shrugged his shoulders.

"I dunno, I guess we just like each other."

"Don't you like anyone else?" Mrs. Pepperdine inquired.

She attempted to pull some information from him by leading him on. "Don't you like Billy Johnson or Sadie Plummer?"

He shrugged his shoulders again, "I.., guess.., Sadie is ok.., for a *girl*," Clarence finally admitted.

"What about Billy Johnson, don't you like him?"

Clarence's shrug and slight turn of his head without speaking was enough to tell her his answer.

"Is anything wrong?" Maude Clearwater asked. "Is Clarence in any kind of trouble with Billy Johnson?"

"Oh, no, nothing is wrong, that I know of."

Again Mrs. Pepperdine went on talking.

"Clarence is one of my best students. It's just that, he and his two friends actions make me feel,.., uneasy."

"His *two* friends? He only has *two* friends at school?" Maude asked.

"And which two friends would they be, Johnny Rivers and Bettie Latimer?"

"They are the only two kids I ever hear about at home but I hoped he had more than two friends at school."

Clarence offered no new information that Mrs. Pepperdine didn't already know. And in her mind the meeting concluded without learning one little shred of information from Clarence that helped clear up the mystery that plagued her mind.

The next visit was with William and Minnie Rivers, Johnny likewise had taken a note home asking for a home visit. At seven o'clock Emmet and Claudia knocked on their front door and were ushered inside.

They, like the Clearwater family, knew Mrs. Pepperdine and had talked briefly about school functions but never a sit down visit like this one.

Emmet introduced himself to William and they were soon exchanging thoughts about their work day. Claudia, or Mrs. Pepperdine in her teacher role for the sake of Johnny's presence, easily talked with Minnie Rivers. Emmet was just along for moral support and knew his wife would get to the matter of the visit in her own good time.

When she fixed her eyes on Johnny he knew it had come. There was something about her eyes that were both pleasant but penetrating when fixed on her subject. He guessed that was the teacher role he didn't see at home and was glad he didn't have to set in her classroom.

"Johnny, ever since your first day of school when you and Clarence Clearwater got into a scuffle with Billy Johnson, I've noticed that you, Clarence and Bettie Latimer are always together. You don't ever play with the other kids nor do they play with you three."

"Why is that?" She asked.

"Why don't you ever include anyone else into your circle of three friends?"

Like Clarence, Johnny shrugged his shoulders at Mrs. Pepperdine's question.

"I dunno, I guess we just like each other."

"Don't you like anyone else in your class?"
"How about Billy Johnson and Sadie Plummer?"

"They are in your class too, don't you like them?"

She asked the same question as before trying to find out what it was about Billy they didn't like.

Again Johnny shrugged, "I dunno, I guess Sadie is ok..., for a *girl*."

"What about Bettie, she's a girl, and you like her?" "Or hadn't you noticed?"

She asked before catching the implication she inferred but went on. "Is there something different about Bettie?"

Johnny had never really thought about Bettie in terms of being a girl at which time his face turned a little pink.

"Is there anything you'd like to tell me here at home? Anything I could do for you at school?"

Johnny felt embarrassed at the question, his face turned red, but didn't know what to say so he shook his head no.

"Mrs. Pepperdine, is anything wrong? Has Johnny caused any trouble for you?" Minnie Rivers asked.

"Oh no." And once again Mrs. Pepperdine found herself reassuring a concerned mother.

"Nothing is wrong.., that I know of. Johnny is a very good student." "It's.., well.., he and his two friend's actions just make me feel..., *uneasy.*"

"Uneasy, in what way? And which two friends do you speak of, Clarence Clearwater and Bettie Latimer?"

"Those are the only two I ever see or hear about at home but I thought Johnny would have more than two friends at school."

She looked at Johnny in a questioning way but didn't ask and he didn't offer anything more. He appeared as *inflexible* as any of his ancestors might have been. He could have been Chief Stonewall Face.

Again nothing new was learned at the River's house that helped Mrs. Pepperdine understand why these particular three kids were so tightly bound together. They could have been secret agents of the FBI or railroad. Neither of the two boys offered a single clue as to their actions and she only hoped Bettie's visit would be more profitable.

John and Belinda Latimer were newcomers to the community and Mrs. Pepperdine had only met Belinda at the beginning of Bettie's first year. It was a brief encounter but pleasant, and then only in passing at school events. She knew Mr. Latimer was a serviceman and spent much of his time away from home.

With Bettie being the odd one of the trio Mrs. Pepperdine hoped to find out what held their friendship together. Why did she prefer the friendship of two boys instead of another girl her age like Sadie Plummer?

Was it Bettie? She wondered. Was she the glue that kept them together? If so, she was a persuasive little lady to be playing such a powerful role. Since Bettie's dad wasn't at home Claudia didn't ask Emmet to accompany her for this visit.

After visiting with Belinda for a while Claudia turned her attention to Bettie just as she had Clarence and Johnny.

"Bettie, it's just us girls here tonight so we don't have to worry about any boys knowing what we say."

"I've been wondering about something and hope you can explain it to me."

"Why do you only spend time with Clarence and Johnny at school?"

"Why don't you spend time with Sadie Plummer, she is a girl like you, in your class, that's your age. Why do you prefer being with the boys instead of a girl?"

For a fleeting moment a thought passed thru Claudia's head, "Does she think she is a boy?"

Bettie's only response was that she liked Johnny and Clarence and didn't like Billy. Sadie was ok but she liked being with Johnny and Clarence better.

"They are my friends. They don't bully me like Billy Johnson."

Mrs. Pepperdine looked at Belinda.

"So Billy bullies you. Is that why you don't like him?"

Bettie's, "I guess so," told her more than she had learned from the other two visits. It was more than just a preference of friendship; they were protective of each other and sticking together made them feel safe.

Belinda wasn't like the other mothers wondering if Bettie had caused her any trouble at school. The "I guess so," answer Bettie gave revealed that she wasn't the trouble or the glue of the three; not just to Belinda but to Mrs. Pepperdine as well.

"Oh, dear," Mrs. Pepperdine had suspected as much but hoped bullying wouldn't be the problem. She knew something had to be done and thought about a fourth home visit.

After she left the Latimer house she prayed, "Lord, You know all things, please watch over these kids and keep them safe."

Chapter Twelve

Most of the time, it seemed, Johnny and Clarence left it up to Bettie to look for some new risky venture. Not that they couldn't think of anything to do on their own; it was just different having her with them. Unlike Bettie, they were born in Pembroke and knew about everything their ten year old minds had been allowed to take in. They knew all about Silver Creek, playing in the wooded area next to town, where all the hideouts were at in case of a fight. They had walked around the ball field and watched as the new high school was built on the second floor of the elementary school building.

    School had started and this was their fifth grade. Since the cooler weather had turned the trio's interest from playing in the creek every Saturday they needed a new direction. After being cooped up in school all week and a couple of

Saturdays of cookie baking lessons they wanted to get outside.

"Let's go for a walk thru the woods that's in back of my house," Bettie suggested.

"We haven't done that in a long time, we might find a bear or where your great grandparents used to hideout from soldiers."

"But remember, my mama said we couldn't go very far into the woods. She'd skin me alive if she found out that I did."

"I ain't never seen no one skinned alive before," Clarence said to Johnny. "Lets go."

"Naw," Johnny answered. "Her mama wouldn't really do it."

"And there ain't no such place in these woods," Johnny declared.

"Or we would know, wouldn't we Clarence?"

He asked for his friends assurance of being right and Clarence nodded, "He's right."

But on a Saturday morning, the middle of October the three of them went running from Bettie's house with a lunch sack Belinda made for them. She never knew when to expect them home so the sack lunch was just her way of sharing the day with them.

She still thought about herself and Abigail at that age having tea parties and were so thrilled when their daddy came home. Charlotte was only a baby.

"Come sit with us, Daddy," she always said.

"We have tea and cookies, Daddy. Would you like a fresh cookie, we just made them this morning?"

Daddy's face would brighten at the sound of his girl's voices calling him to have tea. And without fail he would take a few minutes to spend with his girls. Those were the best memories, of being a young girl. Not a care in the world, not a worry nor a need, daddy took care of everything.

Now Belinda understood his protective nature. Bettie was with her two best friends and as far as she knew there were no dangers lurking about to harm her daughter, but still she always signed a deep breath of relief when Bettie returned.

What Belinda didn't know was that Billy Johnson and one of his friends had been watching Johnny and Clarence after leaving the Latimer house. Though he was only a ten year old boy he had been born with a spirit bent on meanness. From the day Billy was born Irma Johnson had tried to teach Billy the *Christian* way of being honest and fair, loving and kind, and a caring attitude toward every living creature.

"Even a snake or a bug has feelings," she told him over and over. Only, to her dismay, she would find Billy playing with a mouse he had cut the legs half off of or a bird with its wings cut off. She couldn't understand how he gained pleasure from seeing another creature suffer. But it didn't matter to Billy what or who it was, he just liked to make something or someone suffer.

Even though Belinda's sister Charming had come close, she had never thought of a child, even a ten year old, as being anything but an innocent child. Charming was conniving but still innocent in her thoughts.

Belinda didn't know Billy's dad or what kind of man he was. She had no reason to think unkindly of the man. She had met Billy's mother and found her to be a Christian, she even invited Belinda and Bettie home after church to have Sunday dinner.

After meeting Irma Johnson Belinda assumed her husband was also a good Christian man. Not until years later did she learn Billy had a father/teacher that taught him none of the fruits of the Spirit of love, joy, peace, longsuffering, gentleness, meekness or faith.

Instead Henry Johnson taught his son to get whatever he wanted any way he could get it and that was just what he was trying to do. At this age, he didn't know why he wanted to be friends with Bettie Latimer, he just did. And that made disliking Johnny and Clarence easier. He disliked anything that stood between him and what he wanted. And they were always with her.

Well, today, he and his friend Jack Henderson were watching as the three Indian braves set out to explore the back woods. They had explored the woods before and knew where they could jump Johnny and Clarence. *Lickitysplit,* or *lumberly,* in their case, they ran another way to get ahead of the three and hide until they came by.

"With Jack's help, today will be the day," Billy thought to get even with Johnny and Clarence for all the times they kept me from being friends with Bettie.

They found the perfect place to hide behind a big Oak tree and a bunch of Hazelnut trees. They waited and listened thinking that Johnny and Clarence would come that way. But after an hour of waiting Billy and Jack couldn't stand still any longer and decided to go looking for them.

As they made their way on up the hill Billy remembered there was a huge rock at the top. When they came into view of it there Bettie sat, alone, as if she was waiting on them. Billy didn't see Johnny and Clarence so he mistakenly assumed they weren't there.

"Hi, Bettie," Billy and Jack both called to her. "Are you out here all by yourself?"

Billy talked as they continued making their way toward the rock. Bettie just looked at him with *disdain* and let a moment pass without answering.

Then she stood with arms outstretched and began to recite a poem.

"Will you walk into my parlour," said the *spider to the fly,* She was reciting the poem by Mary Howitt. Mrs. Pepperdine had the class learning it but Billy didn't like poems; and she knew it.

"Tis the prettiest little parlour that ever you did spy," She went on. *"The way into my parlour is up a winding stair,*

And I've a many curious things to show when you are there."

"Oh, no, no" said the little fly, "To ask me is in vain, for who goes up your winding stair can ne'er come down again."

Billy interrupted, "Oh yeah, I'll come down."

Bettie went on.

"I'm sure you must be weary, dear, with soaring up so high,

Will you rest upon my little bed?" Said the spider to the fly.

"There are pretty curtains drawn around, the sheets are fine and thin,

And if you like to rest awhile, I'll snugly tuck you in."

"Oh, no, no," said the little fly, "for I've often heard it said,

They never, never wake again, who sleep upon your bed!"

"Stop with the poem" Billy shouted as he and Jack climbed to the top of the rock. But just as they did Bettie slid down another way while Johnny and Clarence walked up beside her. She turned to Billy and Jack after moving away from the rock, and flung her arms wide as the buzzing little fly and then added her own line to the poem.

"Now that you are on top alone, see if you can dodge this stone."

And after her added line let a rock fly thru the air aimed at Billy.

"Owe, that hurt Bettie Latimer," he hollered.

"Or fly away, fly away, fly away home," she said and flapped her arms up and down like a butterfly while swinging herself around.

"Or for all I care,... stay there."

Johnny and Clarence both doubled over with laughter as Bettie made a fool out of Billy and Jack. The three of them walked away from Billy and Jack that day leaving them standing on top of the rock swearing revenge. Johnny and Clarence knew Billy and Jack might be right behind them and tried to think of a place they could all hide out but didn't know of one.

As if they were in no hurry to leave they walked a short distance until out of sight of the big rock then ran to the first hiding place they saw behind an outcropping of rocks. All three flopped down on the ground behind the rocks and the boys looked to see if Billy and Jack were following them. Bettie was first to look up under the rock overhang and see an opening big enough they *might* crawl into.

"Look," she said and hit both boys shoulder before pointing up.

Not sure what they had found or whether they should venture inside they all questioned what it could be.

"It could be a Badger's den," Clarence was first to suggest.

"Naw, Johnny disagreed, it's not clean enough. Nothing very big has been going in and out. Help me dig these leaves back and I'll go in and see."

"Be careful Johnny, Bettie worried, you might get stuck."

Johnny was first to crawl into the hole they'd found, correct that, Bettie found. Lying flat to the ground Johnny wiggled his body into the opening that became a large room.

Johnny thought they had found a cave in the hill that was forgotten or never known about. Apparently, no one now living in or around Pembroke, not even their dads, was aware of it. It certainly wasn't being used by anything except bats and a few rodents.

"Come on Bettie," he said not very much above a whisper. Not sure who he thought would hear him but still talked in a low voice like someone was nearby.

She was second into the cave and Clarence followed as if waiting to see her safely inside. Like two Indian braves always on alert for the squaw accompanying them. With no light to see what the cave held they didn't venture but a few feet from where they crawled inside. Bettie thought about the spider and the fly and wondered if they might now be the fly crawling into the spider's web.

It was cool, damp and eerie feeling, none of them wanted to go any farther without a light. They weren't sure how to make a light but thought a candle would help. All three decided it wouldn't do to tell their parents about crawling into a cave so it had to remain their secret.

"My mama has some candles put away, I'll sneak one out," Bettie said.

"Naw, better not," Johnny thought. "She will know one is missing, mothers are like that."

"Yeah, Clarence agreed, my mama always knows when I sneak something out of the house."

"Well, then I'll take a nickel to the store and buy one."

"Naw, better not, Johnny cautioned again, she will wonder where the nickel went and if you tell her you bought a candle she will want to know what you did with a candle."

"Johnny's right, Clarence conceded again, mothers are *tricky*."

It was one of the few times the boys disagreed with her ideas. They were usually agreeable with her and didn't really care what they did as long as it didn't get them into trouble.

They'd done everything a kid could do around Pembroke, Kentucky and showing a newcomer like Bettie around was more fun to them. But here they were for the first time in a cave they didn't know about. Finding an unexplored cave was a lot more fun than chasing after Billy Johnson.

"Ok, have you guys got a better idea; we are in the dark here?" Bettie was a little impatient with Johnny and Clarence, they struck down two of her ideas and hadn't come up with a better one.

"Maybe we could build a fire inside," Johnny said eager to find a solution and explore the cave.

"I can get a couple of matches from my mama's match box. She'll never miss two matches."

"Good idea," Clarence agreed. "The next time we come you bring the matches, and we won't let Billy follow us again."

"Let's sit down and eat our lunch before we leave the cave," Bettie told the boys.

"We can sit right here where we can see outside, and I won't be afraid."

The next day was Sunday and they all knew they would have to be in church with their mamas not letting them out of their sight. The day after that they'd be back in school all week before another Saturday.

All that week the cave was on their mind more than their school work. They were as jittery and jumpy as three frogs with a hungry snake looking for its dinner.

They thought the week would never end and early Saturday morning Johnny and Clarence were at Bettie's house anxious and impatient to get started.

"Good morning boys," Belinda called to them. "You are here early, did you eat your breakfast?"

They nodded their heads without uttering a word. "What do you have planned today that you are out so early?" She crossed her arms and took a stoic stance as she looked at them.

"If I didn't know better I'd guess you three are up to something today."

Belinda raised one eyebrow, "I have some warm cookies just out of the oven, could I interest you brave Indians in one?"

If a warm cookie didn't interest a boy she knew they were definitely up to something. And when Johnny and Clarence both looked at Bettie before giving their answer, she knew she had her answer; but what was it?

****

After the boys ate the warm cookie offered, and felt they had satisfied Belinda, they casually left the house as if they hadn't been sitting on a match for a week. Bettie walked the same casual walk out of the house behind them and waved a good-bye to her mama.

They were pretending they had all day to kill but as soon as they went around the house they took off running. Belinda watched the sneaky threesome from a window and wanted to follow but instead decided to pay a visit to Minnie Rivers and Maude Clearwater. Maybe one of them would know what their kids were up to.

Neither of the mothers knew but both thought their son had acted secretive all week.

"If they aren't back at one of our houses by noon, Belinda stated, I think we should go in the direction I saw them leave."

Since there were no phones and no one with a car Belinda and Minnie walked back home to wait for the twelve o'clock noon hour and see if they showed up. When the hour passed and Minnie and Maude knocked on Belinda's door, she was ready and waiting.

"I hope this isn't a silly mother thing I've talked you into," Belinda confided. "But Bettie is acting more like a boy than a girl."

They walked toward the wooded hill behind the Latimer's property following the path the kids had taken. The climb up the hill wasn't as easy for them as it was for their kids but they thought something was going on they should know about.

Before they reached the top where the big rock lay Minnie was first to stop and smell the air.

"Do you smell anything?" She asked.

"Like smoke."

They all sniffed the air, "Yes," Maude answered and then Belinda too smelled the smoke.

"What are those kids doing? How did they start a fire?" Minnie wondered. Just then Belinda spied the big rock with a trail of smoke soaring up beside it.

"Johnny," Minnie Rivers called her sons name. Then Maude called for Clarence and Belinda called for Bettie but not one of them answered.

When they reached the big rock smoke appeared to be coming out of the ground.

"The fire is not here, Maude declared, so it has to be from under the hill. They have found a cave under the hill and have lit a fire inside."

"Oh, Lord, don't let it fall in on them," Belinda cried. "How do we find it?"

"There has to be some rocks down around the hill someplace that has an open hole for them to crawl into," Minnie shouted.

Come on let's look around the hill for the rocks."

With all three mothers looking for the same thing it didn't take them very long to find the rocks and see more smoke emerging from the hole.

"Johnny, Clarence, Bettie," they all shouted toward the small hole they could see under the overhanging large flat rocks jutting out.

A minute later Bettie's smudged face appeared and then crawled out. "We found a secret cave, Mama. No one has been in it for hundreds of years, maybe even thousands. Just wait till you see what we found."

Johnny and Clarence both slid out then and they all showed their mothers the arrow heads they found. "There's a lot more stuff inside too, come and see." The boys were sure their mothers would want to crawl inside and see it too.

But all the mothers wanted to know was, if their children were ok, and if there was anything still burning inside to set the hill on fire.

"No, Mama," they all answered at once. "We could see the smoke going up like in a chimney. And we didn't have anything more to burn."

Clarence and Johnny both said, "We decided to name our cave after Bettie's Indian name and call it the Bettie Silvercreek Cave."

Maude and Minnie both looked at Belinda in a way that spoke volumes.

"Johnny," Minnie said. "Go back inside and make sure the fire is all out and then come straight back."

"We are all going to stop at my house, Belinda told all of them, and have us a little talk."

The three mothers could only be thankful the hill hadn't fallen in on their kids. They all felt a good talking to their kids about doing such things was in order. They all walked to the Latimer's house without much talk and when they reached the front steps Belinda told the kids to sit down.

"Do you kids have any idea what you have done today?" she asked.

"Do you know that you could have died in that cave, and we, indicating the other mothers, wouldn't even have known what happened to you?"

At that point Belinda's voice broke and her eyes filled with tears. She stopped talking and hugged Bettie harder than she had in a long time.

"I'm ok, Mama," Bettie said. "Don't cry."

Belinda took Bettie inside and striped her clothes off for a bath. She put Bettie's clothes out on the back porch to make sure they didn't have something on them to get in the house.

The other two mothers marched their off spring home and told them to strip off their clothes to be inspected for ticks or bites. After the inspection was over they heated water for a bath and clean clothes. None of them were to leave the house until time for church Sunday morning.

Chapter Thirteen

During Bettie's bath she asked, "Lots of people will want to come see our cave, won't they Mama?"

"Bettie, I don't want to talk about that cave, I don't even want to hear about it. You could have all been killed in there."

Bettie thought her mama's imagination was running a little wild and when Belinda followed up with,

"There could have been a bear in that cave, or a mountain lion," it seemed to Bettie that she wasn't thinking too clearly. Bettie was afraid she was going to be banned from ever going on long walks with Johnny and Clarence.

"Mama," she said careful of her words.

"The hole was barely big enough for us to crawl in. I don't think a bear or mountain lion could have been in there."

"I don't care if they couldn't get inside, a snake could have been waiting to swallow whatever come into that hole."

"It could have been a hundred years old just lying there getting bigger and bigger off of things that crawled inside. You could be inside that snake's belly right now unable to get out."

"There could have been spiders or bats just waiting to drop on you and bite you. They could have been poison or had rabies. You might be dying right now from some bite and not know it."

And again Belinda inspected Bettie's skin around her neck and hair line for any bite marks.

In Bettie's child's mind she thought it all sounded like a mother's invention of horrible nightmares and thought her mama was exaggerating the possible consequences of crawling into the cave.

She could only say, "Oh, Mama," and went glumly to sit on the front porch *alone*. Without Johnny and Clarence she didn't know what to do but sit miserably on the step, ...so she did.

When they reached home Maude had a similar discussion with Clarence and Minnie with Johnny. For the rest of the day the three each sat alone wondering what the others were doing. But when the men came home from work and heard about the kids finding a cave in the hill they were as excited about it as the kids and wanted to go see it too.

George told Maude, "I'm going to go get William and see that cave. Come on Clarence."

At the same time William told Minnie, "I'm going to go get George and see that cave, come on Johnny and show us where it's at. I've lived here all my life and played thru those woods as a kid. If there is a cave there I want to know where it's at."

Minnie nor Maude could stop their husband so they joined them and all walked toward the Latimer house. They even picked up half a dozen more men and boys along the way. Billy Johnson was among the crowd looking smugly at Johnny and Clarence as he walked with the men. Bettie was sitting on the front porch steps and saw them all coming.

"Mama, Mama," she hollered. "People are already coming to see my cave." When Belinda came to the door to see what Bettie was excited about she was surprised to see Maude and Minnie coming again.

They both gave Belinda a shrug and pointed to their husband. "They wanted to see the cave," Maude said. "And we couldn't stop them," Minnie finished.

Up the path they all went behind the three kids who acted as if they hadn't seen each other for a week. They all talked and laughed about finding a secret cave that no one else knew about.

"We'll be famous," Clarence declared. "Just like Daniel Boone crossing over the mountains."

After George and William saw the open hole they went after shovels and found that over years of time, fallen tree limbs, leaves, and dirt washed from above the rocks had all but filled the opening and hid its existence. George and William dug out enough debris to allow people to easily walk into the cave's entrance.

Bettie's excited voice announced it was the beginning of what *could* be hundreds, even thousands, of people coming to see her cave every year. But as soon as old man Hawkins, who owned the land, heard about the cave he came and built a fence around it and called it the Hawkins Cave.

Mr. Hawkins brought lanterns in for lights to see the inside, better lights than their fire or candles. But their fire had done one thing, the smoke discovered another air passage other than the entrance. The lanterns light did reveal pictures and drawings on the walls that couldn't be seen before. Pieces of pottery, arrow heads, spear heads and other traces of Indian life of years gone by lay around the walls.

Word spread of a new cave being found that brought one visitor all the way from Louisville, Kentucky; an expert in *spelunking* (cave exploration) to see the Hawkins Cave. After he explored the cave and found that it ran much farther, had more rooms than anyone ever guessed, and an underground stream running who knows where, Mr. Hawkins started charging everyone a nickel to see inside his cave.

When the three kids told Mrs. Pepperdine about the cave she wanted to take all of the school kids and sent notes home with each one asking their parents permission. When the day came not only were the students there but they had all brought at least one of their parents. Mrs. Pepperdine wondered if they had misunderstood her letter.

Old man Hawkins allowed the school kids in without charging but suggested the parents could leave him a donation for the group. Some dropped a walking liberty half dollar or two quarters into his box.

After the excitement of the cave wore off and winter weather set in there wasn't much left to do but attend school for a few months. Winter in Kentucky didn't bring hard, cold temperatures that lasted long enough to freeze solid over Silver Creek. A thin layer of ice over shallow water but not enough to be safely skated on. The only thing left for them to do was hope for a deep snow to slide down hill on their sleds.

When the winter's dreaded cold was finally over and the school year ended the kids felt like they had been couped up in the schoolhouse for ever. The last day of school they left running for home, like they hadn't been home for a year. Mrs. Pepperdine drew a deep sigh as she watched them all leave, running as if they were running *from* her. She didn't really think so, or at least hoped that wasn't true. More than anyone knew, except

Emmet, each year she poured her heart into these children as if they were her own.

Summer's fun passed all too soon, for everyone; especially school kids. And with summer's end came the beginning of school again. Mrs. Pepperdine was always as anxious to see all of her students come back as they were *loathing* to sit in their seats all day. It amused her to think of herself as, "The Old Woman who lived in a shoe."

A Mother Goose story by Thomas Newbery. But she taught it to every first grade student and then throughout the school year heard it repeated time after time.

****

There was an old lady who lived in a shoe.
She had so many children, she didn't know what to do.
She gave them some broth without any bread;
And whipped them all soundly and put them to bed.

Year after year she watched to see if the relationship with Johnny, Clarence and Bettie was the same; if they were sticking together like glue. Four years they had been inseparable, it made no difference what Mrs. Pepperdine planned she couldn't get them separated. All five of the same kids that started school together were still in school and each year she had organized in-school projects in an effort to draw them together as friends.

In their fifth grade they were ten going on eleven years old and with Christmas coming soon she planned a Christmas program for the parents and thought of a way she could get them separated. One day she announced the parts that Johnny, Clarence and Billy were to be the three Wise Men and Bettie was to be Mary.

Immediately Johnny and Clarence said, no, they weren't going to be Wise Men with Billy. If Bettie couldn't be the other Wise Man then they weren't going to be either.

"Ok," she held up her hands, in exasperation, "I'll change it. Bettie can be the other Wise Man and Sadie can be Mary. Billy, you can be Joseph."

She felt like throwing her hands up in the air and saying, *"Ok, ok, I give up, you win."*

Or something else real un-adult/un-teacher like, *"What's the matter with you three, can't you see there are other kids to be friends with?" "Can't you see that you are driving me crazy with your actions."*

Ever since her visit with Bettie's mother she had known about the threat Billy posed as a bully. Daily she had kept her eye on him during recess time in hopes of stopping his bullying tactics. More than once she called him inside to sit in his desk while the others continued to play. She told him over and over that his actions toward other students were not acceptable, but he never seemed to change.

It was the most frustrating situation she had ever encountered as a teacher. The other three weren't doing anything wrong and Billy didn't want to do anything right; she found herself right in the middle. But why wouldn't Johnny, Clarence and Bettie interact with other kids?

She gave up trying to *separate* them, for any reason. All summer they run together, played, wrestled, romped and she had heard they still went skinny dipping together at the creek. If *Bettie's mother* knew and didn't put a stop to it, what could she do as a school teacher?

Chapter Fourteen

Summer 1911, they were 12.

Belinda thought only one thing kept Bettie from being the perfect child growing up. A perfect companion to a young mother while her husband was away for years at a time serving his country as an Army officer. But try as she might, she couldn't keep her daughter at home with her as much as she wanted. She, as most mothers, wanted to teach her daughter how to sew, cook her mother's favorite foods, how to keep a house for her husband to be. What motherhood and being a wife meant to a young girl.

But from the time Bettie started school she ran and played with her two best and only friends Johnny and Clarence. That was the fall of 1905 when the boys first started looking out for her, as if they were her brothers. It started when Billy Johnson pestered her the first day of school to get Bettie's attention and then grabbed her wrist. For a first grade boy, pestering and picking on a girl, might have seemed to be a *normal young boy* thing. Just trying to get the attention of a girl in the only way he knew how. But as the years passed Billy continued his *un-normal* actions.

Anyway, Johnny and Clarence didn't see it as being normal and immediately became knights in shining armor to protect Bettie Latimer, yet unknown to them, from Billy Johnson. It was Clarence who first plowed into Billy and then Johnny joined in to let the mammoth Billy know he was to stay *away* from her.

On the outside their relationship remained unchanged all thru school. She chased after those two boys like she was a boy and thought she could out run or out wrestle either one of them. Any other boy as well, for that matter, if she chose to. Anyone that is, *except* Billy Johnson, and she refused any attention he ever tried to give her.

****

Bettie Latimer, almost a young lady but not quite there, sat with her mother in their living room at Pembroke, Kentucky. It was rare for Belinda to have her company alone. Although she was Belinda and John's only child most days it seemed Belinda had two boys as well as a girl, or none at all. Johnny Rivers and Clarence Clearwater were her constant companions.

If they weren't at Bettie's house they would be at the Clearwater or Rivers house. Since the beginning of school Belinda had banded together with Minnie and Maude to keep an eye on their kids. None of the mothers completely understood the relationship the boys had with Bettie but they all wondered if it was because their children was an only child. None of the kids would open up to anyone. Moms, Dad's, and school teachers all felt the same bewilderment about why those three had banded together.., to the *exclusion* of others.

What kept them together, was everyone's question. Belinda didn't mind Johnny and Clarence, they both were mannerly, had good parents and behaved much as if they were Bettie's brothers. Belinda had wanted other children but it didn't happen, it almost seemed they were the two boys she always wanted.

As Bettie grew Belinda informed John about Bettie spending all her time with two boys.

"I don't like it John, Bettie is growing up and should have a girlfriend. She is going to be grown up one of these days. Do you still want her to be running and wrestling with those two boys?"

"Why John, she wears bibed overalls and is still going skinny dipping with Johnny and Clarence? What in the world would people in town think if they knew we allowed her to strip her clothes off and go swimming with those boys?"

"No one knows or cares what they do out here." "The kids will know when it's time to stop, she will grow up one of these days and you will have worried yourself over nothing. Let them have their fun while they are kids, at least they aren't *bothering* anyone."

Truth be told, most of the people of Pembroke knew all about how they run together all summer and were *bothered*. They felt it would lead to no good.

"It's shameful, I tell you, simply shameful the way that Latimer girl runs with those two boys," Mrs. Brierwood told her friend Mrs. Edging who told her friend Irma Johnson. Irma was also friends with Belinda who tried not to add anything more to the already scandalous talk about Bettie. Irma was almost thankful her husband wasn't at home very often to hear the talk and have Billy thinking thoughts that he shouldn't.

But just as an infant learns to say mine and clenches it tiny hand around things it has no need of, Billy fantasied about just one person. He happened to see Bettie with her two comrades heading for the creek one day and ran to see what they were doing. From the first time he saw them all undress before jumping in the water he watched and waited for another time to see Bettie. He told all his friends about what he saw so he could brag, but *secretly* he just wanted to be a part of their little group.

****

But this day the two boys had gone with their dad's on a long fishing trip to the Green River and Bettie wasn't allowed to go. Not that she didn't want to go but this time Belinda said, "No Bettie, this is the men's day, and they are staying over night, you need to let them be alone."

Bettie had told the boys she would catch the biggest fish and that was why she wasn't being allowed to go along. They only laughed at her and hit her on the shoulder as if she was another boy.

"Yeah, yeah," they both said.

Neither of them had ever thought of her as anything other than one of the gang. From the time they all started first grade they had been her protectors. Not because she was a girl, she was just a scrawny kid that needed their help. That day was the beginning of the unofficial, closed to other member's gang, that Bettie more or less, was the unofficial leader of throughout the rest of their life.

That was six years ago when they started school, Bettie was twelve this summer. She sat with her mama watching her knit a baby outfit for her friend Dottie who was expecting a new baby real soon.

"Mama, she asked, why don't you have a new baby? Dottie is having one, the mail man's wife is having one, and our preacher's wife is always having a baby."

"Gobs of mothers are having babies, why don't you have a new baby too?"

"Why, Bettie Latimer, what a question to ask your Mama. Have you kids been talking about babies, if you have cut it out right now?"

"No, Mama," she answered, embarrassed now at her question.

"I only talk to Johnny and Clarence and they don't know anything about babies."

She thought about her answer.

"But, they did tell me they saw some puppy's right after they were born. And baby chicks breaking out of the egg shell."

Mama, is that how people babies are born?"

"Why all this interest in babies, did Mrs. Pepperdine talk to you girls about babies at school?"

"Just once, she said at first a baby grows inside its mother and then God lets it come out. Is that what happens Mama? Did I start living inside you? If I did how did God get me out?"

"I must have been awful little to have been inside you, did daddy know I was there?" "Did he look for me and wonder where I was hiding?"

Belinda's face turned a little pink at Bettie's questions not having gone this way before. But she knew all too soon her innocence would be over.

Belinda knew, even if Bettie didn't, the time of her womanhood was drawing near.

"Let's wait another year Bettie dear, then we'll talk about babies."

Bettie thought her mama was good at putting off questions she didn't want to face, and today Belinda didn't want to think about her baby growing up. Bettie had been her sweet baby and always a delight to have nearby. With John being a military man and away much of the time, Bettie had been a special baby to have; and keep her company during the long periods of John's absence. Now, she could see the years were slipping by all too soon. Belinda looked at her daughter.

"Twelve years old, she mused. "Why, that makes me thirty. How did *Bettie* get to be *so old*, how did *I* get to be *so old*, so soon?"

Belinda thought back about the first time she had seen John and smiled. Why, it could have been only yesterday. She could still see every handsome, rugged line of his face, his close trimmed hair and blue eyes, every detail of what he wore. What he said and the way he spoke. Her insides were in a turmoil she'd never felt before. She thought sure her heart would melt.

"Mama, what are you smiling about?" Bettie asked.

"Oh, just *silly* things a mother thinks about sometimes when they start getting old."

"What kind of things, Mama? What kind of silly things do mothers think about?"

Belinda *blushed* at her question feeling a little awkward. Trying to tell her about her own feelings as a young, unmarried woman was not comfortable.

"Please Mama, tell me what you were thinking about? Tell me what just made your face turn red?"

****

Belinda looked up from her knitting, "It was about your daddy." She smiled again.

"What about daddy? What were you thinking about daddy? Tell me Mama, tell me."

Belinda blushed again and sighed deeply, "Your daddy came right up to my daddy's buggy just as if he was an old friend of the Eisenhall family. With a sweep of his hat he bowed deeply. His words were as sweet as honey as he said,

"Good day Mrs. Eisenhall, and a very pleasant day to you too, Miss Eisenhall."

His blue eyes sparkled and he spoke with a smile to melt any girl's heart. "He spoke to my mama but never stopped looking at me."

My daddy always said, "The Eisenhall girls drew young men like flies to molasses."

"So it was no surprise to my mama when John seemingly appeared out of nowhere."

Only it was no accident that John Latimer approached them that day. For *two years* he had watched, waited, and yes, even prayed, from the window of the barber shop as the Eisenhall buggy came into town full of beautiful women.

John said; "A man had to be *blind* to miss such a sight."

Belinda's mama was the *beautiful* and *elegant* Etolia Henshaw Eisenhall that looked every bit as young as her oldest daughter, Bettie's Aunt Abigail.

Etolia, with a tint of *sandy red* hair piled high on her head, wore matching hats, gowns, gloves and shoes found only in the finest store for ladies wear.

Exhibiting all the graces of a Southern Belle, beautiful, gracious, body erect sitting gallantly beside her husband. She alone was enough to bring attention to the Eisenhall buggy.

Then Abigail was a *reserved* belle too. A young lady in her own right, tall, hair dark as a raven like their father's. Always immaculate, without even trying. She shared the best of both their father's handsome features and their mother's beauty. Especially when they were all dressed for Sunday church.

Etolia looked at Abigail with pride but also a certain *envy* of her youthful beauty that was so easy for her. One might have thought she was dressing for a ball instead of Sunday church. Her beauty stunned most young men into silence which was fine with her.

Belinda was two years younger than Abigail, just coming into young womanhood, not fully aware of how attractive she had become to young men. Her long *auburn* hair in curls under a stunning new hat made her unknowingly attractive.

"When John saw Belinda dressed in one of Topeka's finest dresses for young ladies, he thought she had to be the envy of every single, young lady in town."

"If an undesirable young man approached her all she had to do was look away and it stopped them dead in their tracks."

Thirteen year old Charlotte could have been eighteen because of her charming ways. She was only five years old when their daddy dubbed her charming. She could have talked him into giving her half of the bank. The nick name stuck and from that day forward she was known as *Charming* rather than Charlotte. It so fit her distinctive mannerisms she could have been the oldest of the girls rather than the third.

She once had a young man thinking she was eighteen until her daddy approached with, "I see you have met my fifteen year old daughter Charming."

With her long blond hair she was going to be as beautiful, no, already was as beautiful as her mama or Abigail. They couldn't tell her that at her age though or she would have been driving them all crazy with;

"Can I wear your hat, Belinda?"

"Can I wear your old dress, Abigail?"

"Mama, would you fix my hair up like yours?" "Mama this, Abigail that. Belinda, would you help me make the front of my dress look fuller like yours?"

****

David Eisenhall couldn't have been more proud of his wife and family, but now eight year old Deborah and five year old Ethan were the only small children left. He absolutely adored Etolia and never stopped being thankful for the day they met.

He treated her as if she was a royal queen. He loved all four of his beautiful daughters and was so proud when each one was born. But when his son Ethan was born it was like icing on the cake; his family was complete.

The day John Latimer saw David Eisenhall enter a store and leave Belinda and her mama to wait outside alone he knew this was the opportunity he had been waiting for, his prayer was answered.

John didn't have much to offer but his handsome youth, albeit that was enough for Belinda. She didn't care what he had or didn't have, he was so *devil may care* handsome she wanted to climb right out of the buggy and walk away with him that very day. Her face burned with embarrassment, she tried not to look but couldn't resist a quick glance at his devilish blue eyes.

He didn't have time to ask her or she might have gotten out right then. But when her daddy came out of the store to find John standing near his buggy he was none too happy. He wore a scowl on his face that told John he shouldn't be that close and quickly moved back.

David Eisenhall was eager to see his grown daughters married to a good man but he was so very protective of them. When it came to Etolia, or his girls, David was like a wild stallion protecting his herd. He would have fought to the death to protect them.

"Good day to you sir," John said promptly to avoid any awkward silence. "A very fine buggy you have sir. I was just admiring the fine stitching and leather seats."

"I saw what you were admiring, young man. Don't make yourself out to be a liar if you ever want to court my daughter."

"Why don't you come for supper where you can make a proper introduction of yourself?"

"Daddy..," Belinda said. "I don't even *know* this man."

She whispered to her daddy, red with embarrassment, but John was given the invitation and he was there on time. Truth be known he had waited for an hour just down the street out of sight of their house. Nervous as a cat but more anxious than a boy waiting for a bowl of ice cream.

David Eisenhall had told all of his girls to not even think about a boy until they were *eighteen* and then they could invite a man to their house for dinner. "Any courting would be done on the *front porch.*"

Their daddy still held to some of the old country's ways even though he was an American born Jew. Grandpa Eisenhall was a German born Jew but David was proud to be American born. Even so, Grandpa instilled in David to hold to some of the old country's ways. One custom that goes back centuries, and one David still believed in, was that the *oldest* child should marry first."

Soon, Abigail had to find a suiter their daddy approved of.

Chapter Fifteen

"Did she Mama, did Aunt Abigail find a man Grandpa approved of?" "Who did Aunt Abigail meet that changed her mind about getting married?"

"She doesn't have a husband now, Mama. What happened to him Mama, where did he go?"

Belinda shook her head at Bettie's questions. "Do you ever have just one question? Your mind must run like a race horse, when it starts it never wants to stop."

"My mama used to tell your Aunt Charming the same thing," Belinda told Bettie.

"Oh, Mama, Bettie moaned. "Tell me, what about Aunt Abigail?"

Belinda eyed Bettie and a long sigh came from deep within.

"It hadn't been long," Belinda began. "Before your Daddy made his bold move to know me that Michael Hatfield watched as the Eisenhall family rode into town one Sunday morning."

"He was utterly and completely amazed at the buggy loaded with *beautiful, frilly* women. He watched as we all made our way into the First Presbyterian Church and determined to start attending that church the very next Sunday."

"Abigail was twenty already but had not been in a hurry to jump at the first opportunity of being courted. Plenty of young men had tried but after seeing she was not easily persuaded, soon gave up their pursuit."

"Our father had even invited a couple of them home for Sunday dinner. But when the front porch, on separate seats, was *as far as, or as close to,* Abigail as they could get, they didn't accept another invitation."

Belinda said, "Daddy had his ways of weeding out the men he didn't approve of without having to tell us girls."

"My mama said Abigail was a lot like her Grandma Henshaw, hardworking, stubborn to the bone, and not easily moved."

Belinda went on. "No man had truly interested her until she met Michael Hatfield at church. She didn't know he was there just for that reason but soon found she liked him."

"Since Abigail was oldest and I was now eighteen with Charming thirteen looking like eighteen, our Daddy wasted no time inviting Michael Hatfield home for Sunday dinner."

"That was only six weeks before John made his audacious move to meet me and readily accepted Daddy's invitation."

"Since neither of the two young men were daunted by having to spend an afternoon on the front porch of the Eisenhall house, he approved of them both."

"For the next two years the Eisenhall family entertained Michael Hatfield and John Latimer nearly every Sunday for dinner after attending church at the First Presbyterian Church. After dinner an afternoon of courtship followed on the front porch."

"After a year of courting, and Abigail being already twenty, and Michael Hatfield showing every indication of being interested in marriage, she was allowed to go for long walks away from the house."

"For me, the front porch was as far as I was allowed for another whole year. It wasn't until after two years, of front porch courting, John was allowed to escort me to a church function for young people where he stole his first kiss."

"I tingled from the top of my head to the bottom of my feet. At that instant I knew for sure he was my one true love."

****

In February of 1898 the USS Maine was sunk in the Havana Harbor and the United States was sending men into Cuba to drive out the Spanish who controlled the Western hemisphere island. When Michael heard about the call for men he knew he had to go help.

It had been nearly two years after they first met when Abigail agreed to be his wife. In March of that same year they announced their wedding to be in April 1898. For the next month the Eisenhall house was a flurry of preparations just as if it was totally unexpected.

After two years of courting one might have thought between Abigail and her mama all the preparations of dresses, cake, party and guests would be ready in a moment's notice, but not so.

It seemed a million things had to be planned, a dress had to be purchased, and not from a Topeka store; Etolia planned a week long trip for her and all the girls to go to Kansas City, Missouri where she would buy the finest wedding dress money could buy.

Early flowers like Crocuses and Irises were beginning to bloom in their flower gardens, a climbing rose bush was in full bud the day the wedding was held in the Eisenhall families' back yard. Grandpa and Grandma Henshaw were there along with a hundred other members of the elite families of Topeka.

The wedding day went without a hitch due to Etolia's planning and close eye on every detail. David stayed at work longer hours than usual that month. He didn't want to see his daughter wed to a man, but even more than that, he stayed clear of

Etolia's plans. He knew how she thought and planned every detail and every day made his own plans to steer clear of her as long as possible. It was Etolia's time to plan the wedding arrangement for their daughter.

Michael and Abigail Hatfield were wed in the most stylish manner Topeka, Kansas offered. Tom and Doris Hatfield, Michael's parents, but also among the elite families of Topeka, paid for their honeymoon trip to see the Rocky Mountains. They stayed in one of Denver, Colorado's finest hotels for a week before returning home.

Michael and Abigail returned home with plans to temporarily rent a house in Topeka while Michael continued working with his dad in the canning business. He had already been working there but wasn't settled on what he would do. His dad hoped he would continue working with him in the canning business and David wanted him to start work with him at the bank. In their enthusiasm to help Michael neither of the men had really bothered to ask Michael what *he* wanted to do.

A few days after their return home all of Etolia's perfect plans, for a perfect wedding, to start a perfect life for Abigail were upset when Michael announced to everyone that he was enlisting in the Army.

For the first time ever, Abigail fell apart. Her whole world stopped turning just when she thought it was turning only for her. Never before had she known a tragic or heart rending event in her life.

Her daddy always took care of any problems, all the girls had to do was look pretty for him and he was happy.

But Abigail was married now and this was her problem. Her new husband leaving her to join the Army was almost more than she could bear. She didn't want to share his love with the Army or his country. David had shielded Etolia, and all of his girls, from facing any heartaches so this was new to Abigail.

She had always been in control of her life, her emotions, but in her heart she knew Michael wouldn't return to her. She knew if he went to Cuba that he would die there. She wasn't one given over to hysteria but that day was different. She fell at his feet crying, begging. Clinging as a small child being torn from its mother. Etolia's heart was torn for her daughter, Charming and Belinda were both in tears as they watched Abigail grasp for Michael's consideration.

"Michael, don't leave me so soon," she begged. "If you go to Cuba you will never come back to me. You will be *killed*, I know it, I know it, I know it. You will be killed."

"And for what? What noble cause will you have given your life for?"

"Will *your* death save America? Will *I* be better off because of your death? Will *anyone* be better off?"

"Michael, I've never begged anyone for anything but I'm begging you now."

"Please don't leave me."

"Michael, we were just married, even God doesn't expect a man to leave his new wife until after a year."

Her words made him feel shame at hurting her so. He never intended to hurt her or anyone else. He was as good a hearted person as ever lived. But after she said the words he knew his mama probably felt the same way as Abigail, that he would be killed; and for what? He knew then he should have waited until after he enlisted, after he returned from Cuba, to purpose marriage to Abigail.

Her words made it doubly hard for Michael to carry out his plans. He had not seriously considered being killed, not coming home. He didn't want that to happen but now that Abigail had said it he couldn't get it off his mind. Would he be killed? He wasn't afraid of death he had made *peace* with God a long time ago, he knew for sure whenever his life ended his soul would go to be with God in Heaven for all eternity.

But he wasn't ready for that just yet, he loved Abigail. And no matter what work he did he wanted them to spend the rest of their lives together. Working side by side thru the good times and bad. He wanted to see children born, one or a dozen he didn't care, and then grandchildren and great grandchildren.

Being newly married to Abigail, leaving her nearly tore his heart out but Michael felt an obligation, an urgency to enlist and go fight for America to remain strong. Strong from any European influence. His daddy had been in the Army, his grandfather was an officer in the Confederate Army, not favoring slavery or secession, but the free will of every citizen and every state. His Great Grandpa Hatfield was a boy during the Revolutionary War; playing the drum and sometimes helping the wounded. Michael would be a forth generation wartime soldier.

As much as he wanted children he told Abigail they should wait to start a family until after his return. "If I should die in Cuba I don't want to saddle you with raising a child alone," he told her.

She would have, selfishly, *yes selfishly,* done anything within her power to stop Michael from leaving. But Michael had made his decision, and when he made a decision it was as good as written in stone. When he boarded the train bound for Florida, then to Cuba, Abigail waved her last goodbye to Michael. In her heart she knew she would never see him again.

All the crying, all the wanting, all the praying didn't stop him from leaving her. It didn't stop the obligation he felt to go nor the bullet directed at Michael Hatfield. He died in Cuba leaving Abigail a childless widow, still mourning her loss until this very day.

He wrote her one letter from Cuba in which he poured out his love for Abigail. Line after line was filled with words of his devotion, and passion for her and for life. But on other lines he told her he was happy he could be there and fight for his country.

"It takes men like myself, he said with a foreboding note, if necessary to give my life for America. To keep America free and strong for our children to come."

"How could I ever tell our children I refused to fight for America's freedom?"

"For their freedom."

It was only two weeks after his letter arrived that a telegram from the U. S. Army arrived. Michael Hatfield had been killed during the Battle of San Juan Hill. My deepest sympathy and regrets to the Hatfield family. Signed, Theodore Roosevelt.

Weeks after the news of his death Abigail grievously mourned her loss. Living back with her mama and Daddy after Michael left, she stayed in her room for days unable to face the others.

"God, why did he have to leave me? Why didn't *You* watch out for him in Cuba? Why didn't *You* keep him alive and bring him back to me?" "Why, God, why?"

The questions rang out over and over, her anger could be heard throughout the house, but after the sound of her own voice was gone, all was quiet; no quiet or thundering answers came from God.

When she tired of asking and crying she became infuriated that God was silent and seemingly didn't care. Didn't care that Michael had died needlessly. Didn't care that his death left her alone. Didn't care that she was a twenty three year old childless widow.

The one man she had loved, the one thing she held most dear to her heart was gone. She cried, she pleaded and asked God *why* He let her beloved die. And then one day it struck her, as surely as a lightning bolt strikes a tree, she was putting her love for Michael ahead of her love for God.

Still angry though, she picked up a shoe and flung it against the door. Then another shoe. She went to her chifferobe and pulled out boxes of shoes slinging shoe after shoe, throwing them as hard as she could at the solid oak door.

Through the house they all could hear her shoes banging against the door but no one tried to stop her. When she was thru slinging her shoes the door looked like she had been hitting it with a ball bat.

When her rage subsided she picked up all her shoes and placed them back in the chifferobe. Howbeit, some had broken heals and scuffed toes. She straightened her hair, washed her face and went out to meet the rest of her family.

"*Forgive me God, for acting so childish,*" she said.

Chapter Sixteen

Summer 1911

After Belinda told Bettie about her Aunt Abigail she stayed around home more than she had since she started school. She wasn't sure why, she just did. But gradually she returned to her old self with Johnny and Clarence while Belinda watched *her* little girl slip away from her.

Bettie had always been a good girl, Belinda was proud of her in spite of the fact she spent all of her time with two boys. She just wished Bettie was more feminine; like her and her sisters. Belinda thought she was a pretty baby, but what mother doesn't think their baby is a pretty baby?

All through Bettie's grammar school years she was a regular tom boy always spending time with those two boys, Johnny Rivers and Clarence Clearwater. If the boys went skinny dipping in the creek, she jerked her clothes off and jumped in too.

If they went fishing she did too. If they played ball she hit as hard and ran faster than either of them.

There were times when Belinda wished for a more *serene*, a more *refined* young lady but on those rare days when John was home he'd say to Belinda;

"She is just a kid, let her play with her friends and have fun her way."

But on those days when Bettie came home after being in the water Belinda would say to her,

"Bettie Latimer!" "What do you think the neighbors would say if they knew you went skinny dipping in the creek with two boys?"

"Oh, Mama," she would say not wanting to hear another lecture about spending too much time with her two best school friends Johnny and Clarence.

"They are my only friends and who cares what the neighbors think!"

Belinda Eisenhall Latimer, being from the very influential Eisenhall family of Wichita, Kansas and married to then Captain John Latimer did care what the neighbors thought. She was concerned about her daughter's reputation as well as that of the family. But at times like this it was *not* always clear whose reputation was at stake, Bettie's or the family name?

From the time they started school Johnny, Clarence and Bettie were nearly inseparable, like an exclusive club with only three members. All three mothers, Belinda, Maude and Minnie tried to no avail to persuade them to have other friends. They even tried having birthday parties and invited other neighborhood kids, but no one ever came. It was always just Johnny, Clarence, and Bettie.

At twelve years old they were no longer little kids satisfied to play in the yard and in sight of one of their mothers. Belinda, as well as Minnie, and Maude, all wondered where their child had gone and who these big kids were that invaded the house on occasion. No matter which house they were at all three of them walked inside as if they were at home; and all three mothers welcomed them as if they all belonged to her.

Usually it was just long enough to get a drink of water and pick up a cookie or sandwich; then be off again. "Those kids," all three mothers would murmur while shaking their head.

"I don't know what they do all day so Lord please watch over them."

But when the mothers thought about it, when had their kids been satisfied to play in one of their yards. When had they ever really known what their kids were doing until it was after the doing. From the time they started school they had run around the neighborhood together looking for things to do.

Some days they spent all day looking up and down the banks of Silvercreek for that keg of silver; Bettie just knew that if the legend was true they would find it. But when they tired of searching the banks and found nothing but an occasional snake or frog, the next day they went looking for an eagle's nest. And then there was the day they found a long lost cave together. With their adventurous minds none of the three mothers could keep up with them.

But one Friday, on a hot summer June day, Belinda was almost ready to put a stop to their wandering when Bettie came in the house filthy dirty. And she was dirty too; from head to toe. Her overalls, Belinda bought her so she could dress like Johnny and Clarence, looked like she had been rolled in the dirt. And then water poured on her and rolled in the dirt again. Her hands, arms, shirt and even her hair was sweaty and dirty. Belinda took one look at her bedraggled looking daughter and sent Bettie straight to the bath room to take a bath.

"And put on clean clothes too, a dress this time," she reminded the poor *waif* of a girl who had come into her house. After Bettie returned and looked more like the child Belinda knew, still shaking her head she asked,

"What on earth have you been doing to get so dirty? From the looks of your clothes you have been rolling in someone's garden."

"Oh, no Mama," Bettie was quick to tell her. "We've been picking *baccer worms* off of *baccer plants* for Mr. Browning. Baccer plants, that's what *he* calls them Mama."

"He said he would pay us a nickel for every row we pick the worms off of and he'll *give* us all the worms we want to go fishing too. But we have to look real good and find all the worms or we don't get paid."

"That's what he said Mama, a whole nickel."

"It's real easy to see the worms Mama, they are fat, juicy green worms; Mr. Browning showed us."

"All we do is pinch their head off and drop them in a can, just to be sure they are dead."

"Johnny, Clarence and I each did one row today, see here is my nickel. Monday we are going to start earlier and do two rows."

"Now we can go to the store and buy a bottle of soda pop anytime we want."

Johnny and Clarence both had similar stories for their mother which called for a meeting of the mother's minds. Belinda took Bettie to Clarence's house, it was closest. Then with Maude and Clarence they all went to Johnny's house to see Minnie.

Belinda was in hopes, with Maude and Minnie's help, they could head this thing off before it went any further; but as with most things in the past the kids won out.

"Do you really think picking worms off of tobacco plants is anything for a young lady to be doing?" She fretted and looked to Maude and Minnie for support who for some unknown reason didn't seem quite as concerned.

"Let's give them a day or two," Maude said. "After they've done two rows a few times they may decide on their own to stop."

"I agree with Maude," Minnie decided.

"I understand why you wouldn't want Bettie working in a tobacco field but maybe it won't last long."

"Yes,.. well maybe." Belinda still wasn't happy to think about Bettie picking worms off the baccer plants, as Mr. Browning had called them, but reluctantly gave her approval for them to try it again come Monday.

"But, I don't even know Mr. Browning or where he lives," Belinda fretted.

"He's a real nice man, Mama," Bettie assured her. "His baccer field isn't very far away, just on the other side of Silvercreek."

On their way home Belinda looked at her twelve, soon to be teenage daughter and wondered if she would ever learn the graces of a real lady. Working in a baccer field was no place to learn how to set a table or entertain the company of a young man. She thought about her sister Charming at that age and wished Bettie could have seen her then. At thirteen Charming wanted to wear a pretty dress and look like she was eighteen.

Surely, Belinda thought, she had let Bettie run wild too long and would never get back the young lady she wanted her to be. But then Bettie entertained two young men every day, maybe she did have some of Charlotte's charm after all.

After that first day they worked two more weeks for Mr. Browning until all his baccer field was picked of worms and they were more than ready to be finished. The ten dimes and one nickel they had earned didn't look like very much after ten days of back breaking work. At the end of each week they treated their selves to a bottle of soda pop at the grocery store. Johnny and Clarence both liked Hires Root Beer but Bettie liked Orange Crush. Anyway, Johnny and Clarence both traded her for a swig from her bottle so she could share the taste of Root Beer.

At the end of the second week after their bottle of Root Beer and Orange Crush was purchased they were left with nine dimes and one nickel which seemed like a lot less than when they first started picking the baccer worms for Mr. Browning.

When Bettie went home at the end of the second week she said,

"Mama, if it's all right with you I'm going to sleep late in the morning. It's Saturday and I don't want to see another green baccer worm for a long time."

"Of course it is Bettie dear, sleep as late as you want. I don't expect Johnny or Clarence to be up very early tomorrow either."

Bettie got her bath and thought her pajamas never felt so good. It wasn't long after supper that she headed off to bed without being prompted. Her back was hurting from all the bending over the plants and her neck smarted red from the sun. She wished she had broken a piece off of her mama's Aloe Vera plant and rubbed the juice on her neck.

As soon as her head hit the pillow she was asleep only to start *dreaming* about baccer worms. At first they were the normal size they had been picking off the plants for Mr. Browning. But as she started pinching their heads off each one looked at her as if daring her to try. Then in her dream the worms started getting bigger, the longer she worked the longer the worms became.

Soon they were six inches long and looking more like ground puppies, that were sometimes plowed up in gardens, than baccer worms. They snapped at her fingers when she pulled them off the plants. When she tried to pinch one's head off it bit her finger. Bettie screamed out.

"Johnny, Clarence, *it's biting me, it's biting me, get it off, get it off.*"

Belinda heard her scream and came running to find Bettie sitting up in bed broke out in a cold sweat.

"What is it dear?" She asked.

"It was biting me, Mama, like a snake."

"What was biting you," Belinda asked.

"A baccer worm Mama. The baccer worms got bigger and bigger until they started biting at my fingers. When I tried to pinch one's head off it bit my finger and wouldn't let go."

"Then while it was hanging on to my finger I saw other worms on other plants stick their heads up, smile and then cheer for the one hanging on to my finger."

****

Somewhere along the way Belinda and John failed to see Bettie wasn't that lean, willowy, tom boyish girl of younger years. They continued to think of her as their little girl even when she showed signs of becoming an adult woman.

When they were out playing they all three took their shirts off to be cooler. In their younger years the boys never noticed Bettie looking any different than they did. But Bettie's chest had started getting bigger than theirs and they couldn't help wondering why.

Johnny and Clarence continued to be her knights in shining armor, no other boy ever dared come close to her when they were with her, which was almost all the time. If the boys wanted to play ball they were always considerate of her and ask, "Bettie, do you want to play ball?"

If they went for a walk one would always ask, "Bettie do you want to go along with us?"

Every year since they were six years old, until the summer they were *thirteen*. If one of the boys thought a dip in the swimming hole sounded good they didn't have to wonder if Bettie wanted to go along. Of course she wanted to and stripped her clothes off just as fast as either of them. They would jump in the water naked as jay birds and play until they were worn out. This was their private place, *they thought.*

They *thought* they could go off by ourselves, as they always had, with never a concern that anyone might be watching.

Chapter Seventeen

Summer 1912

Before school was out they all had their thirteenth birthday and this summer was going to be different; it was an awkward point in their lives. No longer young kids looking for an adventure but not seen as adults either. They were... just there.

Some days they sat around Bettie's house, then Johnny's, and another day Clarence's house. Each of the mothers recognized this summer was different for them and tried to interest them in helping in their gardens.

One day they all pulled weeds and hoed Belinda's garden and the next day Mrs. Clearwater's and then Mrs. Rivers' but there were still three more days to do nothing. Sunday they knew they would be in church and none of them really looked forward to sitting thru another of Pastor Whetlock's boring sermons about Abraham, Isaac, or Jacob. Not even the little shepherd boy named David who killed the giant named Goliath with a sling shot, or a story of Daniel and the lion's den, held their interest any more. And no one could hardly stand the off key singing of Mrs. Spriggs or the poor pianist Mrs.(missed her note) Townsend.

None of them suggested picking baccer worms for Mr. Browning but after a month of boredom Bettie said, "Ok, you guys, let's go pick baccer worms."

Out of shear boredom they walked the mile out of town to his house. They would have rather gone swimming, it had been fun just stripping off and jumping in, but... Or maybe a hike in the woods, like last summer when they slipped off one day and walked all the way back to the lookout tower. That was one of the days no one knew where they were all day. They watched for a Black Bear and didn't see one but alas, here they were ready to pick baccer worms again.

"Hi Mr. Browning," they all called to him.

"I've been wondering if you kids wasn't coming back this year. I need to get these worms picked off before they ruin my baccer plants."

"You're later than last year, the plants are bigger and so are the worms."

Mr. browning was a kindly old gentleman, always a smile on his face and a funny story to tell his young listeners.

"I have me a baccer dog that used to help me pick the baccer worms off the plants," he told them. And immediately they knew a story was coming.

"*Old Baccer Worm*; that's what I call him. I love that old dog."

"When he was a pup he played around here with me amongst the baccer plants until I dropped one on his nose. He didn't like it and shook if off. After that day every time he saw one on a baccer plant he'd draw his lips back in a snarl and pick it off with his teeth."

"He couldn't *tolerate* the taste of a worm in his mouth and would drop it on the ground so's I could step on it." "But he'd go right back to looking for another baccer worm and pick it off like your mama's pick blackberries."

"Be careful now," Mr. Browning cautioned them. "The bigger worms might bite your fingers."

Bettie saw him smile and knew it was a tease meant for her but he didn't know she had a dream about having one bite her finger. Bettie hadn't forgotten the dream from last year but that was one thing she never got around to telling Clarence or Johnny.

"What happened to Old Baccer Worm," Clarence asked.

"He had to quit coming to the baccer field," Mr. Browning said sorrowfully. "Too much baccer juice the vet said."

"The vet said, If you keep letting him pick baccer worms for you he will die young."

"If he hadn't gotten sick he might still be helping me pick these worms off."

"How old is Old Baccer Worm," Clarence asked.

"Well, let's see now," and Mr. Browning arched an eyebrow in apparent thought back over the years as to how old his dog would be.

"I was born in 18 and 35. I was nigh on to thirty years old when I got him; that would have been in 65 just after the war was over."

"Yep, that's just when I got him, in 65. I guess he'd be about forty eight years old now, give or take a year or two."

"How old are you, Mr. Browning," Johnny asked.

"Well, let's see now;" Mr. Browning arched an eyebrow again and looked at his young listeners to see if they were paying attention.

"I reckon I'd be about ninety nine, going on one hundred this year."

"Mr. Browning, do you chew this Burley Baccer?" Clarence asked.

"Oh, no, I tried putting a leaf in my mouth once and made me sick as a dog, you couldn't pay me enough to do it again. That's why I haven't gone on to be with the Lord, like Old Baccer Worm almost went to his grave early."

"Course he would go to doggy heaven not people heaven."

"If it's so awful, Mr. Browning, why then do you grow it?" Bettie wondered. "If I chewed baccer do you think I would die young like Old Baccer Worm almost died?"

"Likely as not you would," he replied somberly.

Mr. Browning said it so matter-of-factly none of them questioned his sincerity. The interrogation about baccer juice and Old Baccer Worm seemed to be over and they were soon finding the fatter worms on the baccer plants as Mr. Browning had said they would.

Mr. Browning watched them get started until they moved a few feet away but not too far for him to hear Bettie whisper to the boys,

"Mr. Browning is *funnin* us. If he was born in 1835 like he said, he won't be one hundred until 1935."

"And dogs don't live to be *forty eight* years old either."

Mr. Browning could hardly keep from laughing right out loud. At least *she* was listening.

Mr. Browning watched the three of them work across the first row and met them with a water bucket and dipper.

"How's about a drink of water to wash the baccer juice down?" he asked.

"I don't have any baccer juice in my mouth," Bettie was quick to let him know. "I'm not dying young like Old Baccer Worm could have," she said.

Bettie wasn't ready to let his story drop about his dog. She didn't have a dog but she knew from Johnny and Clarence that dogs didn't live to be fifty years old.

"How old is Old Baccer Worm?" she asked again. "You said he would have died young but you call him old, which is he young or old?"

He smiled seeing as how he had painted his self into a corner. "Well, now Bettie," he said to her as he wiped his mouth with his big hand. She thought she saw a brown stain at the corners of his mouth that looked like baccer juice but didn't ask about it.

"Looks to me like we've got ourselves an *oxymoron*."

"A what?" Clarence asked and looked at Johnny.

"I dunno either," Johnny shrugged.

"An oxymoron," Mr. Browning replied.

"What's an oxymoron mean, Mr. Browning," Bettie asked. "Is that like when Johnny and Clarence act like morons?"

"I think it's more like when I say to my wife,

"Miss Lucy, your fried apple pie is *awful good*."

"And they are awful good too. Would you kids like to try one when you get this next row finished?"

"I can tell her you will be stopping at the house if you want me to."

Bettie knew Mr. Browning had *wormed* his way out of telling her how old his dog really was but somehow finding out how old 'Old Baccer Worm' was didn't seem as important as it did before he mentioned the fried apple pie.

It was past noon when they finished that second row of baccer plants and was thinking more about fried apple pie than finding baccer worms, at least Bettie was until Johnny asked;

"You don't reckon any of these baccer worms got to his apple tree, do you?"

"I dunno," Clarence answered thoughtfully. "But if Mr. Browning mentions baccer worms getting into the apples I'm not eating any pie."

"Baccer worms wouldn't be in apples," Bettie told them. "They like baccer juice not apple juice.

"Anyway if one did get in an apple Mrs. Browning would see it."

"You guys stop talking about baccer worms being in the fried apple pie," Clarence complained.

"I want to eat it without wondering if baccer worms are in it."

When they finished picking worms from the second row of baccer plants that day they stopped at Mr. Browning's house and knocked at the back door.

"You kids come on inside;" they heard a ladies voice thru the screen door.

"You can wash your hands in here."

They looked at each other a little uncertain about entering someone's house without them being at the door but they soon knew why. A plump grandmotherly lady with the biggest smile came wheeling herself toward them in a high backed wheelchair. Without the wheelchair she would have looked no different than any other grandmother.

But at first they wondered if she was different and wondered if maybe Johnny's question about baccer worms getting in the apples might be true.

"I'm Miss Lucy, she said; Mr. Browning's wife." "He told me there would be three hungry kids coming in looking for some of my fried apple pies."

"Would that be you three or should I look for three more?"

She laughed knowing they were the ones but it seemed as if it made her happy to have someone to talk to; so she did. She talked and talked...and talked.

"There's the wash pan and a bucket of water right over there; she pointed. When you are thru come on to the table and I'll have each of you a fried apple pie waiting."

She turned the wheelchair around and headed back for the hot stove where all the fixings waited to make the pies. When we returned she said to Bettie;

"You must be Bettie." As if after they washed the dirt off their faces she could tell now that she was a girl; but not beforehand.

"And I'll bet you are Johnny," she pointed toward him. "Mr. Browning said Johnny was the one with dark hair."

"So, that leaves you Clarence, the lighter haired one." "Did I get your names all right?"

"Yes, Ma'am," they all answered her that she was right. "Oh, paw shaw." She said and laughed.

"I'm not Ma'am, I'm Miss Lucy." "Now sit yourselves down here at the table, your pies will be ready in just another minute."

"Yes Ma'.. er, Miss Lucy;" they all stammered.

"Would you like a nice cool glass of milk to drink with your pie?" She asked and wheeled off to get it before they could answer.

"Where is Mr. Browning?" Bettie asked. "We thought he would be here."

"Oh, child he won't be back until evening. He took his old dog and went squirrel hunting. One of them walks about as slow as the other."

"What's his dog's name?" Clarence asked.

Miss Lucy laughed again, "He calls him Old Baccer Worm." They looked at each other and couldn't help wondering if at least one of the Browning's memory was failing.

Bettie knew she wasn't being polite but she couldn't resist asking Miss Lucy. "How old is 'Old Baccer Worm'"?

"Child," Miss Lucy said and threw her hands in the air. She laughed so hard the rest of them couldn't help but join in with her.

"Mr. Browning had that old dog when we got married nigh onto fifty years ago. I think he'll have "Old Baccer Worm buried on one side of him and me on the other side."

Miss Lucy never did tell them how old 'Old Baccer Worm' was but they thought he must be pretty old. If Mr. Browning had his dog when they got married maybe he *was* forty eight years old.

Miss Lucy's fried apple pie was *sooo* good they would have come in for one every day but didn't want her to use up all her dried apples.

As last year, two weeks later they were finished picking the worms from Mr. Browning's baccer field and still nothing to do the rest of summer. After sitting around each of their houses for a couple of days they needed something to do.

****

"I'm sick of doing nothing, let's walk to Hopkinsville," Bettie gave both Johnny and Clarence a shove.

"We can be back by afternoon."

They struck out as if walking five miles there and five miles back was no more than a hike in the woods or along Silver Creek. The summer when they were that charmed age of *thirteen* walking five miles to Hopkinsville and five miles back was like a stroll in the park. But when they returned they were hot and ran to their favorite swimming hole in Silver Creek to cool off. Hardly anyone else ever walked along Silver Creek to see them; so they stripped off all of their clothes as they had done in the past. Only this time Bettie noticed Johnny and Clarence both look her way then turn quickly with red faces. She also noticed a burning in her face she hadn't felt before but the moment passed and they all jumped into the water for their usual rowdy swim, splashing and dunking each other. At the time Bettie didn't understand why neither Johnny nor Clarence wanted to dunk her or chase after her as before.

That was the *last* time they all went skinny dipping together.

From *that* day forward their relationship was different. It was like that day opened their eyes to the difference in their anatomy. The boys no longer wrestled Bettie to the ground and pinned her shoulders down as they had done in the past, they were like the brothers she never had to protect her. She felt safe any time she was with them; to go any place or do anything. No other boy ever bothered her as long she was with Johnny or Clarence. Many times the three of them walked the five miles from Pembroke to Hopkinsville with never a thought of danger.

If anyone observed their actions as being different than before they last went skinny dipping they just commented on their grown up behavior. But the three of them knew they were different; even if no one else could tell. They began to see each other as grown up individuals, not just play mates.

They had become inseparable friends and did everything together since the fall they were six years old and started school. Clarence and Johnny never thought about Bettie being any different than they were. She could out run and out wrestle them or any other boy in school, so why should they think of her as being any different.

"I'm not an egg, I won't break," Bettie said to them more than once.

But during their teen years they began seeing Bettie as different; a lot different. In high school her relationship with Johnny and Clarence remained, to the outsider of their trio, unchanged. They had played together around the neighborhood for so many years, no one gave a second thought about seeing them still palling around together.

But things did change, they were changing even if no one else noticed. The last time they went skinny dipping together not only opened Johnny and Clarence's eyes to the fact of Bettie being a girl but having a close relationship with a girl was different now that they were growing up.

All the years growing up and their wanderings alone, not one time did Bettie, nor Johnny or Clarence, ever take advantage of the other. Rather than looking for an opportunity to take advantage of Bettie they became more protective of her. There wasn't a boy in Pembroke that knew if they ever bothered her Johnny and Clarence would clean their plow.

They never knew that last day they went skinny dipping together there was another pair of eyes watching them. Another's eyes that burned with desire.., and revenge. Not just to be alone with Bettie but revenge against Johnny and Clarence for always standing in his way.

Chapter Eighteen

1912

    That summer the Indian trio thought they had picked baccer worms for the last time. They were tired of picking those worms off baccer plants but there wasn't a whole lot else for growing kids to do around Pembroke, Kentucky.
    If not for Miss Lucy's invitation to come back and eat one of her fried apple pies any time they wanted to it might have been a boring summer. Johnny and Clarence would have gone to see Miss Lucy at least twice a week but Bettie said,
    "No, once a week is enough." "We don't want to wear out our welcome."
    That's what Belinda always told her so she thought it must be true. But Miss Lucy was always just as happy to see them one time as the next.
    "Just the same," she reasoned with them.
    "She should be twice as happy to see us if we only go once a week instead of twice."

Clarence was still hung up about how old Mr. Browning's dog was or if he even had a dog. Every time they stopped by his house to see Miss Lucy for fried apple pie Clarence asked Mr. Browning to see 'Old Baccer Worm'. But every time they were there it seemed the old dog had wandered off some place and Mr. Browning didn't know where he was. Bettie told Clarence to stop asking but this was one time he didn't listen to her and ask anyways.

All the times they picked baccer worms for Mr. Browning Billy Johnson nor his friend Jack Henderson never wanted to help. At least not while they were there. Anyway, none of the three wanted the other boys around, they just wanted to be alone. But where were they was a question in their minds that none of them ever asked.

After they had finished picking baccer worms for Mr. Browning they started looking for something else to do the rest of summer. They were thirteen years old that summer and not feeling like little kids any more.

One day Bettie was so bored with living in Pembroke, and nothing to do, she went to the General Store to ask Mr. Hanks if he could use a good helper. It was then she found out what Billy had been doing all summer, helping his uncle, Mr. Hanks.

She hadn't known before that day that Billy's mother was Mr. Hanks' sister. But later she learned he helped Irma raise Billy since Billy's dad was gone from home most of the time.

Bettie had been in the General Store with her mama lots of times and never saw Billy. She had guessed the lady she saw working with Mr. Hanks was his wife not his sister. But that day Billy was there in place of Mr. Hanks and walked right up to her as if they were old friends.

"Hi Bettie," he said. Then he put *his* hand out and touched *her* arm but she brushed it away.

"Don't touch me," Bettie said and looked him square in the eyes with as much hate as she could muster.

"Don't you *ever* touch me again, Billy Johnson," she said between gritted teeth.

"Get away from me, now or I'll tell Johnny and Clarence to be waiting for you."

Johnny and Clarence had always been the magic words to turn Billy away but with his growing size she couldn't help wondering how much longer it would work. They were all growing up but it seemed that Billy could be at least one or two years older than his age.

"I came in to see *Mr. Hanks*," she said still gritting her teeth. "Not you Billy Johnson."

"Oh, my *Uncle Tom Hanks* isn't here right now, but I'd be glad to help you, Bet-tiĕ."

He said it with a sneer and a grin that she wanted to wipe off his face. If it hadn't been Billy Johnson she was facing she probably would have taken him down right there in the store. Bettie couldn't stand to be near him alone and ran from the store. She heard him laughing as she fled away but she didn't care she had to get away.

"Bye now Bet-tie," she heard him sneer.

Where was Johnny and Clarence anyway? Bettie hadn't seen them that morning and sure would have liked to have their company. She was steaming mad when she got home.

When Belinda saw her stomp in the house she stopped her work in the kitchen and went to see why Bettie looked like she could tear the house apart.

"What's wrong Bettie dear, has something happened?" "Your face is all red."

"Yeah, something happened," Bettie muttered back.

"Billy Johnson was born. And he won't leave me alone."

"Does Billy still bully you?"

"Yeah, Mama," she said forgetting she was supposed to be a young lady with Christian ideals.

"I *hate* Billy Johnson. I *hate* the day he was born."

"I *hate* the day I ever met him. I wish he was dead, Mama, dead."

Right then she wished she had of been talking to Johnny and Clarence rather than her mama.

"Oh Bettie, don't say such things, surely you don't mean them."

"I do Mama, I do. And when I tell Johnny and Clarence about today they just might *kill* him."

"Why don't we sit down and you tell me all about what happened."

Bettie couldn't sit down. As she talked to Belinda she paced the floor with arms flailing about as if she might take off any time. She wished she could *fly*, fly away some place where she'd never see Billy Johnson again.

"He put his hand on my arm, Mama. Just as if he owned me."

"Oh, I can't stand for him to touch me, Mama. Just wait until I tell Johnny and Clarence, they'll rub his nose in the dirt good and hard. And while they are at it maybe they will just kill him too."

"Oh, Bettie," Belinda said trying to calm her daughter.

"Don't talk like that, surely you don't mean it."

"You know one of God's Ten Commandments is not to kill. And Jesus said we are to forgive someone seventy times seven times."

"I think He meant to just keep on forgiving and not count the times someone does you wrong."

"I know all of that Mama, but right now I'm so mad I don't care what God said."

Bettie was still walking back and forth thru the house as they talked, she was so mad she couldn't sit down. If she'd sat down she might have burned a hole right through whatever she sat on.

"Maybe I should have a talk with Billy's mother. We've been friends a long time now."
"Maybe a good mother to mother talk would help."
"It wouldn't help Mama, I know it wouldn't."
"You don't know Billy like I do. He watches and waits until he can't be blamed, and then he does things."
"Things that no *normal* person would do."
"Oh, I can't stand him, I can't stand him, I can't stand him."
It was then that Johnny and Clarence showed up and walked right in the Latimer house without knocking or calling for Bettie. It had been that way for a long time; for all three of them. No matter whose house they were at they went right inside just as if they all lived there and all three mothers were fine with that relationship.
"Hi, Bettie, hi Mrs. Latimer," they both said.
"Where have you two been this morning?" Bettie snapped, not at all in a mood for pleasant conversation.
Without so much as a hello or an answer she whirled around and grabbed them both by the arm.
"Come on you two, we've got some talking to do."
She pushed them both out the door and headed straight for the creek where they could be alone and talk.
"What's the matter Bettie?" Clarence asked and then Johnny asked the same question without

getting an answer. Right on top of the spot where they buried their silver coins Bettie plopped down by the big tree over looking their swimming hole; then she started talking.

"Did you guys know that Billy Johnson's Uncle is Mr. Hanks that runs the General Store?"

She asked both boys at the same time then went right on ranting.

"I was so bored this morning I went in there to ask Mr. Hanks if I could do some work for him. But he wasn't there. And just who do you think was there in his place?"

"Guess, go on guess, who do you think was there?"

But before either of them could answer she blurted out, "*Billy Johnson*, that's who; *Billy Johnson.*"

"Of all the people in the world it could have been, it was the one I hate the most."

"Oooh, I hate Billy Johnson."

"Do you know what he did when I went in the store today?"

She went right on talking without giving either Johnny or Clarence a chance to answer.

"He came right up and touched my arm; that's what he did."

"Acted like we were old friends, more like he owned me."

"You know how he's always bragging about his dad owning his mother? He did the same thing to me."

"I want you two to catch him and hurt him, real bad. I don't care if you kill him."

"Mama said don't talk like that, forgive and forget is the Christian way but I don't feel very Christian right now. I want you to hurt Billy bad enough that he will leave me alone."

Johnny looked at Clarence, "We'll take care of Billy, he said, don't you worry about him no more."

Bettie was so mad she didn't know or care what she was asking her two best friends to do for her, but as always they didn't hesitate to come to her defense. When she had run out of steam they all sat with their backs to the tree. Johnny nor Clarence said anything, they just sat with her in silence.

They didn't know how long they sat like that but long enough for Bettie's temper to leave her. Finally she asked, "What have you guys been doing this morning? Why didn't you come by my house?"

"We were looking for something to do the rest of summer," Clarence answered.

"We didn't think you'd want to go along," Johnny added.

"But I guess we should have taken you with us."

"You know Mr. Teague that lives at the edge of town, we heard about him needing some help stacking his hay. We didn't think you would want to stack hay, but do you?"

"Mr. Teague said he could use another helper if we knew of one," Clarence added.

"It'll probably take us the rest of the summer since Mr. Teague only works until noon. Says his lumbago won't let him work any longer."

"We didn't see his lumbago, why do you suppose it won't let him work any longer if it's not there?"

"I dunno," Bettie said. "But tomorrow morning I'm going with you two. I can stack hay if you guys can."

"I've got an idea, Johnny said. You stay home tomorrow Bettie. Clarence and I will go by the General Store and tell Billy Mr. Teague needs a big, strong boy to help pitch hay up on the stack tomorrow."

"He can't resist showing off how strong he is. We'll only need one day with him and the next day you can go."

Ready to set a plan in motion they all jumped up. Bettie went toward home and Johnny and Clarence went toward the General Store to find Billy.

Chapter Nineteen

September 1912

    This was their last year attending the Pembroke Elementary School; the last year to have Mrs. Pepperdine as their teacher. They didn't know how they had gone thru seven years of school already, but they had. This was their graduation year from the elementary school. After this year was over then they'd go upstairs to the high school.

    Except for the first day of their first grade, every year the first week of school, Mrs. Pepperdine had let school out early to take her entire class to see the show horses. They were beautiful animals, stallions and mares that came from all over the world to Pembroke, Kentucky.

    For the small town of Pembroke, horses weren't the only show that came to town. It took wealthy people to own expensive horses and come to horse shows. For them it was just another outing, another day in the park, another opportunity to show off their wealth before their socialite friends. The younger families with small children brought their nannies, older folks brought maids and butlers. Tents were set up with tables, chairs, fine china, silverware, and cloth napkins. No comfort was spared from those who had money; and lots of it.

The three had asked Mr. Browning about the horses that were brought in for the horse show and he knew all about it.

"I've been going to that horse show for the last sixty five years, maybe more," he told them.

"How old were you when you first went?" Clarence asked. He still wasn't over finding out Mr. Browning's age.

"I was just a little shaver, maybe four or five years old, give or take a year or two."

They had already figured out that they couldn't believe Mr. Browning about his age. At first he was born in 1835 and almost one hundred. Now, he had gone to the horse show sixty five years and that plus being five years old to start with only made him seventy years old. They guessed that was closer to his age than one hundred but still didn't know for sure.

He named several of his favorites and started in like he could see them. "There were Appaloosa, Arabian, Gypsy, Quarter Horse, Belgian, Caspian, Clydesdale, Exmoor, Florida Cracker, Friesian, Haflinger, Lippit Morgan, Missouri Fox Trotter, Mountain Pleasure Horse from Kentucky, a Paint,

Peruvian, Saddlebred, Tennessee Walking Horses, and a Thoroughbred."

"You three kids come and go with me to the horse show and then later we'll watch the people show. It's a sight, I tell you." He laughed and slapped his big hands together.

****

They never told Mrs. Pepperdine about Mr. Browning taking them with him to see the real horse show; and people show as he called it. They weren't sure which fascinated them the most.

Mrs. Pepperdine always enjoyed looking at the beautiful horses as much as the kids. Bettie couldn't help wondering after seeing them so many years if, she might enjoy them *more* than the kids.

Their class still had the same five that started together, Bettie, Johnny, Clarence, Sadie; and of course Billy Johnson. No one had come or gone from their class until this year when Jackie Brookes came to school. Her mom and dad had moved into Pembroke from the country so this was her first year in town.

Bettie had seen her before school started while out walking with Johnny and Clarence; but they passed on by her. They hadn't meant to be snobbish toward her, they were just being their usual exclusive self. By now they thought they were the big kids at school and had forgotten how it felt to be new at anything around Pembroke.

With Johnny and Clarence's help during the last seven years Bettie had learned just about all there was for a kid to know about school. She didn't remember how scared she was of school and wanted her mama to stay with her that first day.

Mrs. Pepperdine introduced Jackie to the school and asked everyone in the room to say hi to her and tell her their name. When it came Bettie's turn she said, "Hi, my name is Bettie Silvercreek."

All the kids except Jackie laughed at her name, but by this time it didn't bother her to be laughed at; she even liked it. She sat back down feeling a little *smug* at her joke.

Mrs. Pepperdine smiled but at the same time frowned. "Bettie it sounds like you are married to that creek."

"Now tell Jackie your real name."

Bettie stood again and said, "Yes ma'am, my name is Bettie Latimer."

Bettie didn't know what got into her that day other than wanting her last name to sound like Johnny and Clarence's names. When she did things like that at home and Belinda scolded her she would say,

"Bettie, that's just plain old ugly meanness working its way out of you."

"That old ugly is working it's self out of you so you can be the prettiest girl in town."

Bettie thought her mama must have told her that a thousand times, or at least it seemed that way. But she didn't feel pretty or care if she was or not.

By then there wasn't a kid in school, or hardly a person in Pembroke, that didn't know she had changed her last name to Silvercreek. Bettie didn't know why it was so important to her that her name sounded like Johnny and Clarence's but it did.

She went nearly all thru school being called Bettie Silvercreek. Some kids like Billy Johnson would say it with a *sneer*; thinking it would embarrass her. But it didn't embarrass her a bit, she liked being called Bettie Silvercreek.

****

Now, on the first day of school starting their eighth grade, they were all a little too big for their own britches. All of them felt a little confrontational from the summer so Bettie tried to blame the hot summer for her *insolence*. At least that's what she told herself and felt satisfied with herself until she heard Mrs. Pepperdine talking again and tried to listen.

"I want all of you to make Jackie feel welcome, Mrs. Pepperdine was saying, and pray for her dad. He had to stop working their farm because of his health."

"If I didn't know all of you kids, and your parents, I wouldn't tell you anything this private. But I've talked to Jackie's parents and they assured me it was quite all right with them to share the reason for their move into town."

"Jackie's father needs to be near a doctor, she explained, they need our prayers and our help."

"And I don't ever want to hear one of you kids say that Jackie is a needy child or I will be very disappointed in you."

"Nothing makes me upset any faster than to hear someone making fun of another person."

Her eyes roamed the classroom trying not to let them land on Billy any longer than anyone else.

While Mrs. Pepperdine talked Bettie couldn't help looking at Billy Johnson too and think about all the times he had pestered her. She wasn't sure if that was the same thing as being made fun of or not but thought it was and wondered why Mrs. Pepperdine wasn't that upset at Billy.

Bettie knew Johnny and Clarence had taken care of Billy out in Mr. Teague's hay field. Billy only worked one day and for some reason didn't feel like going any more so she worked with them every day until the hay was stacked. While she was day dreaming about her problems with Billy she only faintly heard what else Mrs. Pepperdine said until she heard Clarence's voice.

Mrs. Pepperdine had said while she had everyone's attention she would try to answer any questions we might have about Mr. Brookes.

"I imagine some of you are going to wonder about his illness so I will try and answer your questions ahead of time."

"Mr. Brookes was a tobacco farmer until this summer when he fell ill and hasn't recovered."

Bettie looked at Johnny and then at Clarence. They all knew they were wondering about the same thing.

"Was Mr. Brookes going to *die young* of too much baccer juice, just like 'Old Baccer Worm almost died?"

And leave it to Clarence, he still wasn't over thinking about Mr. Browning's dog, 'Old Baccer Worm.' When he shot his hand in the air Johnny and Bettie both knew what he would ask. And moaned quietly.

"Mrs. Pepperdine, is Mr. Brookes going to die young of too much baccer juice? That's what Mr. Browning told us almost happened to his old dog."

All the kids, except Bettie, Johnny.. and Jackie, laughed. Mrs. Pepperdine had to hide a smile but told Clarence she didn't know about Mr. Browning's dog but doubted if it was the same thing that caused Mr. Brookes' illness.

Then she went on to explain. "Mr. Brookes has what the doctors call 'Nicotine poisoning' or 'Green Tobacco Sickness."

"It's caused from handling wet, green tobacco leaves and absorbing the nicotine poisoning fumes from the plants."

"It's nothing to be ashamed of or afraid of. Mr. Brooks was a hard working farmer who harvested his own tobacco plants and came down sick. Jackie won't catch it from him and you kids can't catch it from Jackie."

"Nearly all of us have been sick from something, sometime, and his sickness is no different. So please, forget about the sickness and be her friend."

Mrs. Pepperdine smiled at all the class but for some reason, this time, Bettie felt like her eyes stayed on her longer than anyone else.

Clarence still wasn't ready to let go of his question and continued to talk. Some times Bettie thought Clarence was a little like her neighbor's Bull Dog, when he got an idea in his head he wasn't quick to let it go.

"Old Baccer Worm," he said,

"Could have got wet from the baccer plants, he persisted, and got the Green Tobacco Sickness."

"He used to help pick the baccer worms off baccer plants right along with Mr. Browning."

"And Johnny, Bettie, and I have been picking baccer worms from Mr. Browning's baccer field every summer."

"Do you think we could get the Green Tobacco Sickness?"

All the kids except Johnny and Bettie were laughing at Clarence again for saying baccer worms and thinking a dog could have gotten sick from the baccer plants. And now wondered if they might get sick too. They didn't know if anything Mr. Browning had told them about his dog was true but Bettie wished Clarence would stop talking.

"Clarence, have you been having headaches, sick stomach, not sleeping; anything like that?"

When Clarence said, "No Ma'am, Mrs. Pepperdine," she then assured him she didn't think he would be getting sick.

Then Ed Thompson raised his hand to ask a question.

"Mrs. Pepperdine, I was just thinking." "If a person can get sick handling the green tobacco leaves, why don't people get sick that chew or smoke tobacco?"

"That's a very good question Ed and shows that you are thinking ahead of just today. People that smoke or chew tobacco can get very sick, it's a sickness called cancer, and there is no cure."

"Most people that I've heard about with cancer die within a matter of months."

"I hope you kids, especially you boys, she said and looked at each one of them in the eye; will remember that."

"When you are wanting to do things to look like a man, remember that what you do doesn't make you a man; its who you are."

"Smoking or chewing tobacco doesn't make you a man, and it can make you sick with cancer, and there's no cure for cancer."

Without anyone noticing Mrs. Pepperdine turned from a serious note to a light hearted, happy sounding voice and smiled.

"Now, everyone all at once say, "Hi Jackie," and then we will all say the pledge of allegiance to the flag before we start."

Everyone, but the new first grade students and Jackie, knew Mrs. Pepperdine had her class say the pledge of allegiance to the flag every Monday morning before anything else. As Bettie advanced thru the first seven years saying the pledge made her more aware of what it meant to be an American and she gladly said it.

Mrs. Pepperdine explained it like this. It starts out by saying, "I, and I means me," she said. "Pledge allegiance," give my solemn word, and I do with all my heart.
"To the flag," Old Glory.
"Of the United States of America,"the stars and strips that represent all forty eight states.
"And to the Republic for which it stands," a republic, a free self governing country.
"One nation, Under God, Indivisible, With liberty and Justice for All."

Johnny and Clarence would place their hand over their heart and repeat the pledge of allegiance as if they were already soldiers fighting to protect their country. Bettie couldn't help wondering if they would be real soldiers sooner than they knew.

When Mrs. Pepperdine had everyone's seat assigned she announced it was recess time. As always now, she followed the kids to the door and watched as they went running outside to play. Once again watching, and hoping, to see if Johnny,

Clarence or Bettie would join in a game with the other kids. But, as she watched a deep sigh escaped. Once again she felt she had failed them somehow, when she saw them all walk off from the others, together. Sadie Plummer was the only girl to befriend Jackie.

This was the last year Mrs. Pepperdine would have Bettie Latimer, Johnny Rivers, Clarence Clearwater, Sadie Plummer, Billy Johnson and now Jackie Brookes. She couldn't help wondering if there was something more she could do for them to make them all be friends.

Belinda hadn't walked Bettie to school since the first year she started, after that Johnny and Clarence always showed up at her house in time to walk with her. Every year though on the first day of school Belinda always looked for her little girl, and her two body guards, to get home early and have a cookie and glass of milk.

By the time their second year started their mothers knew their routine and joined forces, a sort of 'mother's allegiance,' against the forces of raising their children. One year Johnny's mother brought the cookies and milk and the next year Clarence's mother would bring them to the Silvercreek house. This was Belinda's turn and all three mothers were at the Latimer house, waiting on the front porch to see them home from their first day at school.

Belinda was first to start the usual motherly questions like;
"Did you learn anything today?"

Bettie said, "No," to her mama's first question.

Then Belinda asked;
"Were there any new students this year?"

"Yes, seven," Bettie answered her second question.

Maude Clearwater tried and asked;
"Did anything different happen today?"

Clarence said, "No," to his mothers first question.

Then Maude asked;
"Is Mrs. Pepperdine still your teacher?"
To which Clarence answered, "yes."

Minnie Rivers tried by asking;
"Was everyone there?"

Johnny said, "Yes," to his mother's first question.

"You three are our kids, aren't you?"

Johnny said, "Yes," again to his mother seemingly unaware of his mother's poignant question.

Belinda looked at Bettie as if she expected her to volunteer some other bit of information on her own. Bettie shrugged,

"That pretty well sums up our day; how about you Mama?" She looked at Maude and Minnie too, to include them in her question.

210

Belinda looked at Minnie and Maude, and then back to Bettie, before answering for all three mothers.

"Oh, we have just been sitting around all day waiting for you kids to get home and tell us all about your first day at school."

Maude said, "Minnie, now that we've heard everything about school we might just as well go home."

Minnie nodded her agreement.

Chapter Twenty

September 1912

All thru each school year Mrs. Pepperdine talked to her eighth grade class on a more adult level than the others. Their Social Studies classes were filled with lessons about current events in Christian County, in Kentucky, the United States, and world; helping to shape their young lives. The past Presidents, Theodore, or Teddy, Roosevelt, William Howard Taft, and now the current new President, Woodrow Wilson, just elected, always made for interesting topics.

It was said that Theodore Roosevelt was elected as a Republican but was really a Democrat. William Howard Taft was a Republican that swept in on Roosevelt's coat tails and now a Democrat President, Woodrow Wilson was elected. War was eminent in Europe and everyone was fearful but hoped the new President didn't lead the United States to become involved.

One day Mrs. Pepperdine stated the obvious to the boys, "You do know that if our new President leads the United States into a *European War*, you boys will all be enlisted as soldiers."

She must not have wanted to think about 'her boys' being sent off across the ocean to fight a European war. After that day she didn't talk about Presidents and wars like she had in the past. It was like *saying it* had made it so real in her mind she didn't want to think that her Johnny, Clarence and Billy might someday go off to war. And she knew more than they did that going off to war meant that, some or all, of them might not come home alive.

The eighth grade was a *good* year for most everyone, the classes were easy for everyone except Billy; even Jackie fit into their class. It seemed like Billy's mind was always someplace other than in school. His dad's attitude of, *get what you want any way you can get it*, always seemed to drive Billy away from simple class work. He had cheated and lied to Mrs. Pepperdine so many times all of the class thought she must be glad to see him finally finish the eighth grade.

Coming to the town school for the first year, from a country school, made Jackie an easy *target* for Billy to take advantage of. All the rest of them were on to him. Until that year poor Sadie had taken the brunt of his pranks since he couldn't get to the famed trio of blood brothers and sister. But now with someone new in class he made poor Jackie's school year miserable.

Had Johnny and Clarence not been so devoted to Bettie they probably would have protected Jackie just as they did her. But things were as they were and none of them wanted anything to change. They didn't know yet just how life would tear them apart no matter how much they wanted to stay together.

Bettie was a tomboy all right, Belinda had given up on trying to change her. She always wanted to wear bib overalls like Johnny and Clarence. Except for her *longer*, auburn hair it was hard to tell her and Clarence apart. Bettie didn't *think* Belinda knew but she kept cutting the ends of her hair off so it didn't get any longer. After she trimmed her hair she'd put it down in her overall pocket then scatter it someplace outside.

She was careful where she scattered her hair she didn't want Belinda to find it, but Mr. Browning gave her another reason to take care where she scattered it. Mr. Browning told them how the hair from a horse's tail would fall into water and become a snake and she sure didn't want to take any chances that her hair would do the same thing. Bettie didn't know if auburn colored snakes would be poison or not but she didn't want to find out.

Mrs. Pepperdine had all of her class perform a Christmas program for the parents and John was home on furlough for a month. Since they were all going to the school Christmas program he wanted Bettie to open her presents early. That year he brought her a new dress, slippers, anklets and all the lady like under things to wear under the dress. He was just sure by now his little girl would have out grown her bib overalls and want some new lady like looking clothes to wear.

Bettie looked at the new clothes and said, "Thank You," to her daddy then hugged and kissed him just like she always had, but secretly she'd rather the dress had been a new pair of overalls. When she didn't run to her room to try them on he pushed her in that direction.

"Go on Bettie, try on your new clothes and let me see you dressed up pretty like your mother."

That was the first time Bettie had ever been made to feel like she didn't look as pretty as her Mama or that she should dress pretty like her. She knew Sadie Plummer always came to school in a dress, and even Jackie Brooks that had grown up in the country, came to school in a dress. Even though Bettie was growing up it never occurred to her that she should dress like a young lady.

"All right, Daddy," she said. "If you want me to I'll put the dress on,.. just for you."

Bettie wore the new clothes all that day and to the school program to satisfy her daddy, but the next day she was back in her overalls. When she saw him frown at her she knew what it meant. It wasn't necessary for him to tell her he didn't like to see his daughter dressed like a boy.

But it wasn't enough to make her want to wear a dress all day. What if Johnny and Clarence wanted to slide down hill in the snow on their sleds? What if they wanted to go for a hike along the creek? She couldn't do the kind of things they wanted to do in a dress.

So she wore her overalls.

At the end of the school year Mrs. Pepperdine made every eighth grade class at the Pembroke Elementary School feel special. As well as all her long talks with them she made one last home visit, just to see the parents. She asked each mother to make their child's favorite treat and if possible both parents come to the school at one o'clock for a graduation party.

The last day of the school year John couldn't be home so Belinda went alone. That morning she made a fresh, double batch of Bettie's favorite Oatmeal cookies.

Johnny and Clarence's dads came home from work at noon to go with Minnie and Maude. Minnie made Johnny's favorite candy; chocolate fudge. Maude made Clarence's favorite; two big pans of cinnamon rolls.

Billy's dad and mother, Henry and Irma Johnson, came for him and brought a big bowl of sliced peaches. Bettie thought Mr. Hanks must have given her canned peaches from the General Store since peaches weren't even set on the tree yet.

Sadie Plummer's mom and dad, Sally and Lucas Plummer both came. Sally Plummer made an angle food cake that went real well with Mrs. Johnson's peaches. Everyone wondered if Jackie's dad and mom would come but didn't want to ask if he was too sick. Then when they came in Thelma Brooks helped her husband Ted, into a chair; a chair beside Henry Johnson. Thelma carried a tin of sugar cookies she said was Jackie's favorite.

The kids all stopped talking for a minute and stared at Mr. Brooks. They weren't sure what they expected to see. Bettie knew what she was thinking, Johnny and Clarence too; especially Clarence.

"How did the 'Nicotine Poisoning' make a person look?"

"Did it make you look funny? If so, how would he look if he had it?"

The next two hours passed all too quickly. They all enjoyed eating all the favorite sweet desserts their mothers brought. They all laughed and talked more freely than they had all thru school. For once in Bettie's life, if she hadn't really known Billy, she might even have talked to him. Before, every time when she *had* to talk to him she ended up shouting at him. She guessed it was because their parents were nearby that he didn't try any of his dumb tricks.

Bettie didn't know until it was too late to duck out of school and run for home but Mrs. Pepperdine had one more surprise waiting for her graduating class. But when she saw Mrs. Pepperdine step up behind her desk and clear her throat, she had a sinking feeling that something unpleasant was going to follow.

"Class and parents, could I have your attention?"

She wore her usual smile but Bettie knew down deep in the pit of her stomach where all the goodies lay she had just consumed, the next few minutes were not going to be nearly as pleasant as the time had been consuming them.

Mrs. Pepperdine went on talking but Bettie was barely hearing her for the rumble she felt in her stomach. It was worse than the fear she felt on the first day of school when she wanted her mama to stay with her. It was worse than having Billy Johnson touch her and make her skin crawl. It was worse than the fear she felt when they first crawled into an unknown cave; wondering what was inside. It was even worse than picking baccer worms off baccer plants for Mr. Browning and the dreams of having them snapping at her fingers.

When Bettie heard Mrs. Pepperdine say, "Will all of my eighth grade class please come *forward*," she knew, for sure, she wasn't going to like what followed.

They all took one look at each other and knew they'd much rather be outside playing dodge ball or dare base. Anything but going up to Mrs. Pepperdine's desk. Even big, rough and tumble Billy Johnson turned a little green and would rather have been elsewhere. Whatever Mrs.

Pepperdine had planned for them they knew they didn't want.

Mrs. Pepperdine went on talking.

"Since I have been your teacher now for eight years, well, all of you except Jackie," she corrected herself.

"I want each of you to think back and tell me, and your parents, what stands out in your mind that you've learned since you started school."

Her class all gulped and wondered what they'd learned. Their stomachs churned some more on what they had just been eating. Bettie sat there as if she was glued to her seat, she couldn't move.

What did Mrs. Pepperdine expect them to say? Something their parents could smile at and say how proud they were of their child? Something dumb sounding like, "I've learned my ABC's?"

Bettie could even say them backwards; if she wanted to. Or, "I've learned to count to one hundred." She guessed she could do that backwards too; if she wanted to.

Maybe she could say, "I've learned the multiplication tables," or "I've learned to identify all forty eight states of the Union on a map."

"I know the pledge of allegiance to our country's flag, I can say President Lincoln's Gettysburg address, I can say the preamble to the constitution."

Her mind raced thru the last eight years of school as if it was on speed dial; only there wasn't a speed dial. But it could have been wild horses though, galloping across the western state of Montana. Her mind ran over a million things they had talked about in school yet she couldn't think of one thing to say.

Then to her horror she heard Mrs. Pepperdine's voice break into her semi-conscious mind. Only this time Mrs. Pepperdine wasn't just talking, she was calling Bettie's name. Her, Bettie Latimer Silvercreek. Mrs. Pepperdine had finally called her Bettie Silvercreek and her mind was frozen in space some place. Bettie felt embarrassment rise to her face knowing she was calling her name and she just sat there like a bump on a log. She realized her brain must have been frozen just like she was frozen to her chair.

Just then she felt Johnny take hold of her right arm and Clarence take hold of her left arm; they were propelling her forward with them. Her mind refocused just in time to hear Mrs. Pepperdine say again, "Bettie, I'd like for you to go first."

Chapter Twenty One

Summer 1913

Bettie lived thru near mortification that day. It was almost as bad, no I think worse, than it had been her very first day of school. Now, as always school was out before the end of May and she had three long months ahead of her with nothing to do.

She was fourteen years old, out of grade school, and not a little kid any more. Making cookies with her mama didn't hold the appeal it once did. As the thought crossed her mind she realized it had never held much appeal to her. Bettie only did it for her mama's sake, or Johnny and Clarence.

This summer she was as tall as Belinda but when she was grumpy her mama didn't fail to remind her that she was still mama and Bettie was her little girl. Belinda and John were still just Mama and Daddy; only older. John had been in the

Army fifteen years and been sent to England and then to Germany before he would come back home.

This summer Bettie hoped he could come home, she longed to see her own Daddy. She hoped he would still love her when he saw how much she had grown. She felt tall and gangly, skinny as a 2 x 4 board without any of the fullness of other young ladies. Bettie hoped he would still see her as his little girl even though she stood as tall as her mama.

Germany had started a European War and Belinda was happy when John came back to the states. Bettie remembered Mrs. Pepperdine talking to the boys at school, reminding them they would be the right age to become soldiers if war broke out. She didn't know what she'd do if Johnny and Clarence entered the Army and went away.

Pembroke was still the *same* little town it had always been. At fourteen she didn't want to walk around town looking for something to do. Bettie didn't feel like going back in the woods with Johnny and Clarence looking for the lookout tower.

There was no keg of silver buried along Silver Creek to look for; they knew it was still buried out back of Whispering Pete's house. His old house still stood where it always had; at least it had for as long as anyone knew. One day Bettie told Belinda it should be made into a *shrine or a museum* ...or something.

"People shouldn't forget who Whispering Pete was," Bettie said with regret sounding in her voice. She walked thru the house talking and flailing her arms as if folks remembering who Whispering Pete had been was akin to remembering who George Washington had been.

"Whispering Pete was a living legend in his own time," she said.

"He was the last Cherokee Indian who escaped the soldiers that were sent to move them from their land."

"If we only had that *keg* of silver some Indians hid along the bank of Silvercreek," Mama said.

"Maybe we could get enough interest from our state government to make his old house into a State Park."

"Cherokee Trail State Park," she said just as fast with no idea where the name came from. It just fell out of her mouth.

"Do you really think so, Mama?" Bettie asked. "I bet if Johnny and Clarence helped me we could go find that keg of silver coins."

Bettie had to *hide* a smile from her mama when she thought about the keg of silver buried behind Whispering Pete's old house.

"He had to be over a hundred years old when he died." But before her mama could ask any more questions about Whispering Pete and the keg of silver she jumped from Pete to another old man.

"Then there was old Moses," she said. Bettie continued to pace the floor and flail her arms about as if she might take off at any moment. Years before, Belinda had told her about the Wright brothers flying machine with a propeller that flew in circles.

"Folks should remember who old Moses Gray was just like they remember the Wright brothers and their flying machine."

"And he didn't really have a last name, he borrowed it from his masta, Mr. Gray."

"He died two years ago. Johnny and Clarence's dads said he was one hundred and ten years old when he died."

The thoughts in her head were all in a whirl and she knew she needed to find Johnny and Clarence. Her arms stopped flailing and she stopped pacing the floor as if they had been propelling her thru the house.

"You know something Mama, the Moses in the Bible was only one hundred and twenty years old when he died; just ten more years than Moses Gray."

"Hey, I just had an idea." "If we could find a white man who had lived around Pembroke during the same one hundred years, we would have a white man, a black man, and an Indian all one hundred, or more, years old."

"Shouldn't that be in some kind of history book, or something?"

"Three different kinds of men, all who lived in Christian County Kentucky, and lived to be one hundred years old."

"Bye Mama, I've got to go find Johnny and Clarence, we have some *serious* thinking to do."

When she rounded up Johnny and Clarence they headed to the bank of Silvercreek where they did their best thinking; by the swimming hole.

Bettie no sooner had she told the boys about her idea of finding a white man that was one hundred years old when Clarence blurted out the obvious name. "Mr. Browning."

"Remember him telling us he was ninety nine years old, and that was three or four years ago?"

Johnny conceded that it would make him over one hundred years old.

"But I always doubted it," Bettie said.

"I always felt like he was putting us on. He told us he was born in 1835 and if he was he'd only be seventy eight, a long ways from one hundred."

"And. if Mr. Browning is one hundred years old he would have been born in 1812 not 1835. I still say he was just funnin us."

"And then he told us he had been going to the horse show for sixty five years that would have made him seventy years old."

"This is 1913 and minus seventy years would make him being born in 1843, not 1835. Give or take a year or two, as he always says."

"Yeah," Johnny agreed with Bettie.

"We don't really know when he was born or how old he is. He always tells us something different."

"Ok," Clarence conceded. "Maybe Mr. Browning isn't one hundred but he might know someone who is."

"Hey, I've got it," and Clarence had another sudden brain storm to set a record.

"His dog, Old Baccer Worm."

"If Old Baccer Worm is fifty years old that has to be some kind of record. Let's go see Mr. Browning and this time we won't leave until we see Old Baccer Worm."

"Yeah, and while we are waiting maybe Miss Lucy would make us a fried apple pie," Johnny said."

"Is finding out how old 'Old Baccer Worm' is and eating fried apple pies all you two can think about?"

"This is a *serious* matter."

They all agreed, *albeit* for different reasons, to go see Mr. Browning and Miss Lucy. In order to get them both to agree to go with her, Bettie gave some merit to Clarence's idea and agreed with Johnny that one of Miss Lucy's fried apple pie's would surely taste good. However, she had no intentions of sitting around their house all day waiting for 'Old Baccer Worm' to come home.

Bettie gave both boys a shove to get them started then jumped up. Being fourteen years old she didn't want or need their help. She was lean and wiry as any boy and didn't let being a girl stop her from acting like one of the boys. They were still *true-blue, tight-as-glue* friends but sometimes she had to give the boys a nudge in the *right* direction to make sure they stayed that way.

****

"Hi, Mr. Browning," they all called when they caught sight of him out back of his house cleaning a squirrel. Clarence thought his chances of seeing 'Old Baccer Worm' increased since it appeared that Mr. Browning had just returned home from squirrel hunting.

"Have you been out squirrel hunting this morning, with 'Old Baccer Worm'?" You could hear the reason for his question in the tone of his voice.

"Hello, Bettie, Clarence, and Johnny." He returned their greeting with a smile and answered Clarence's question.

"No, I found these three squirrels, ma-self. I haven't had Old Baccer Worm to hunt with for.., nigh onto twenty five years, maybe more."

They all three looked at each other in disbelief, or shock, or wonderment at all the things Mr. Browning had told them about his old dog. Bettie tried not to but she felt her head slightly shaking at Mr. Browning's still another version of his dog's life.

"He was a good *old* dog," Mr. Browning went on talking. "He lived to be nigh onta twenty years old."

"He lived to be a ripe old age, but like all of us will;..he died one day."

"I buried him out in the middle of the baccer field with the baccer worms thinking he wouldn't feel lonesome."

"Does Miss Lucy know that 'Old Baccer Worm' died?" Clarence asked.

"Or does she think he's still alive and goes out hunting with you?"

"Well now, I've never told her that he died so I guess she still *thinks* he's alive and goes hunting with me."

"I talk about taking him with me like I still do so Miss Lucy doesn't think I'm out alone. I guess Miss Lucy does think he's still alive."

"And you got him in 1865, is that right?" Clarence asked.

"Yes, that was the year, right after the War."

Bettie looked at Johnny and Clarence as Mr. Browning talked, they all *knew* both stories about Mr. Browning being one hundred years old and 'Old Baccer Worm' being fifty years old weren't true. And with that knowledge she felt the possibility of finding a white man at least one hundred years old slip away.

Johnny saw a tear come to Mr. Browning's eye and thought it would be a good time to ask about Miss Lucy.

"Mr. Browning, Johnny asked, do you think Miss Lucy would make us a fried apple pie? I sure have been hungry for one."

"Next to a young, fried squirrel," Mr. Browning said and held the three skinned squirrels in his hand.

"Miss Lucy's dried, fried apple pie is next."

"Go on inta the house, If she has some she can get us all a fried apple pie done in two shakes of a squirrel's tail."

As they entered the house with Mr. Browning, they all called out a, "Hi," to Miss Lucy.

"Miss Lucy," Mr. Browning said. "I found three hungry kids wandering around out in the woods while I was squirrel hunting."

"Do you think you could fry them a dried apple pie before they starve?"

And again they saw how he liked to tell stories.

"Oh, paw shaw," she said and laughed. "They don't look like they're starving to me."

"But it just so happens that I have a few dried apples ready for fried apple pies."

"If you'll build me a fire in the cook stove I'll hav'um ready in no time at all."

She gave her wheel chair a whirl to the table and started preparing the pie crust for fried apple pies while at the same time hurrying Mr. Browning along to build the fire up.

"Have you kids ever eaten a fried squirrel?" she asked.

Johnny and Clarence both said, "Yes Ma'am," they had.

But Bettie said, "No, Ma'am, Miss Lucy, I've never even seen a fried squirrel."

"Then all of you kids come by at dinner time tomorrow to eat with me and Mr. Browning, and

I'll have these three squirrels fried and ready to eat."

"We'll have fried squirrel, okra, brown beans, and corn bread. I might even have a fried apple pie for desert."

Chapter Twenty Two

When Bettie went home that day she told Belinda about Miss Lucy inviting them to eat dinner with her and Mr. Browning the next day.

"Please say it's ok Mama. She invited Johnny, Clarence and me, and I've never eaten a fried squirrel."

"Have you ever eaten fried squirrel Mama?"

"I bet if I asked him to Mr. Browning would go squirrel hunting again and they would invite you for dinner too."

"Bettie, my Grandpa Eisenhall was a very strict Jew, he would never have allowed my daddy or anyone else in his family to eat squirrels."

"Why not?" Bettie asked. Intrigued.

"He would make you answer your own question by asking, "Do squirrels have split hoof?"

"When you answered no, squirrels don't have hooves."

"Then he would shrug, there is answer."
"God does not allow Jew to eat meat of animal not having split hoof."

"Are you a Jew, Mama?" "Am I a jew?"

"No, Bettie you are not a Jew. Your daddy is a Christian, not a Jew. When I was a girl I was a Jew like my daddy, but now I am a Christian like your daddy."

"Someday, Bettie, I hope you will become a Christian too."

"How Mama, how do I become a Christian? I want to be a Christian like you and daddy."

Bettie was fourteen years old and wondered why she never knew before that day that she was different than her mama and daddy.

"If you was a Jew like your daddy?" Bettie asked. "How did you become a Christian; by marrying daddy?"

"Are Jews different than other people?"

"Bettie, we need to have a long talk you have asked a very important question. Bring me my Bible."

When Belinda had her Bible she turned to the New Testament book of John, chapter 3 and read Bettie a story about a man named Nicodemus. It reads;

"*There was a man of the Pharisees, named Nicodemus, a ruler of the Jews:*
The same came to Jesus by night, and said unto Him, "Rabbi, we know that thou art a teacher come from

God: for no man can do these miracles that thou doest, except God be with him."

Jesus answered and said unto him, "Verily, verily, I say unto thee, except a man be born again, he cannot see the kingdom of God."

Nicodemus saith unto him, "How can a man be born when he is old? Can he enter the second time into his mother's womb, and be born?"

Jesus answered, "Verily, verily, I say unto thee, except a man be born of water and of the Spirit, he cannot enter into the kingdom of God."

"That which is born of the flesh is flesh; and that which is born of the Spirit is spirit."

"Marvel not that I said unto thee, Ye must be born again."

"Bettie, in the old days God *chose* the Jewish people to be His special people; to *reveal* Himself thru them,.. to the rest of the world."

"And because the Jews were God's chosen people they began to think that *just* being a Jew was the most important thing God wanted of them."

"But the Jews were to be a people God could show the world His grace, mercy, and peace. His justice, His protection, His provision. But they are people that do bad things just like other people do bad things."

"So, God sent His Son, Jesus, to tell the Jewish people, as well as everyone else, that they were doing wrong and needed to be saved from their sins in order to go to heaven."

"That is what Jesus was telling Nicodemus when He said, *You must be born again.*"

Later, Jesus told other people, "*I Am* the way, the Truth, and the Life."

"*I Am* the Door that leads to heaven. No man comes to the Father except by Me."

"Bettie, when a person understands that they have *sinned* against God and accepts Jesus as their Savior, whether they have been a Jew, a Catholic, or anyone else, they become a Christian."

Belinda went on talking to Bettie. "I knew I had done wrong things, just like the old time Jews and Nicodemus, and needed to be born again."

"When I asked Jesus to come into my heart and forgive me of my sins *He* made me a new person inside."

"That's how, and when, I changed from being a Jew to a Christian."

"Bettie, do you think you have ever done anything wrong?"

When Belinda asked Bettie that question she remembered many of the things her mama had told her not to do, but did them anyway. But not wanting to admit them to her mama, she felt a little red faced at the idea. So, she asked her, "Do I have to tell you or can I just tell them to God?"

Belinda smiled, "Tell them to God, Bettie, *I, nor anyone else*, ever needs to know." "*He is waiting for you to talk to Him now.*"

"Ask Jesus to forgive you and come into your heart. Promise not to ever do them again. He will hear your prayer."

That was the day Bettie became a Christian just like her Mama and Daddy. Bettie wished her Daddy was home so she could tell him but the Army had sent him to England and wouldn't be home for another year. The next best thing to telling her daddy was telling Johnny and Clarence.

Bettie was so excited to tell them that she was a Christian she went running off to find them. But when she blurted out to them that she was a Christian now they just looked at her like, *she's taken leave of her senses.*

That was one of the first times she had ever talked to Johnny and Clarence when they didn't understand, but she knew she wasn't thru talking to them about it and someday they would understand. They would become a Christian like her.

****

When they were seated at the table with Mr. Browning and Miss Lucy, Bettie was seated between Johnny and Clarence just like she always was; they never stopped being her protector.

Mr. Browning reached out for Johnny's hand, and Miss Lucy took Clarence's hand. He looked Bettie's way,

"Take their hands Bettie," he said.

"Then I'll ask the blessing for this fine dinner *He* has provided us that Miss Lucy has prepared for us to eat."

Inwardly Bettie smiled, knowing she was a Christian now and could give God thanks too.

After the blessing Miss Lucy started talking and Bettie had to stop her musing to hear what she said.

"There are six hind legs, six front legs, and six pieces of back," Miss Lucy said. "You kids and Mr. Browning start with a hind leg, they are the biggest."

"I'll have a front leg," she said. "I like them the best." She went on talking and took two before passing the platter to Mr. Browning. He took a back and a hind leg before passing it on to Johnny.

Miss Lucy passed a piece of cornbread to Mr. Browning and then helped each of the kids get a piece open on their plate to cover with brown beans. Without taking any okra Miss Lucy passed the pan of okra to Clarence.

He only looked at the okra and said,

"No thank you," then passed it on to Bettie. Just as fast she passed it on to Johnny. He looked at it and also said, "No thank you."

Mr. Browning looked at all three of them.

"None of you likes okra!" he said in feigned surprise.

"Miss Lucy doesn't like okra either, but today I was afraid I wouldn't get any."

Bettie watched as Mr. Browning enthusiastically spooned the big slimy looking okra pods onto his plate. They made Bettie think about the big green baccer worms, and then knew for sure she didn't want any. The squirrel leg and brown beans on cornbread looked good, but she wasn't sure which she should try first.

Bettie waited to see how Miss Lucy would eat her squirrel leg before picking hers up. She didn't know if there was a right way or a wrong way, so she waited to watch Miss Lucy. Johnny and Clarence both picked their squirrel leg up and took a bite as soon as it was on their plate; but they had eaten fried squirrel before.

Bettie didn't know Miss Lucy was watching her but she must have been waiting for her to take a bite. For as soon as she did Miss Lucy asked, "How do you like the fried squirrel, Bettie?"

Bettie couldn't think of anything more complimentary to say than, *"Real good."*

And then asked, "Do you think you could fry some more squirrels and ask mama to come for dinner some day?"

Bettie hit one of those times when she couldn't stop talking and some of what she said didn't always come out the way she hoped it would.

"She's never eaten a squirrel,"... "I mean a fried squirrel," she added real quick.

"When she was a girl her daddy was a *Jew*, and Jews don't eat squirrels on the count of them not having a split hoof."

Bettie stopped long enough for Miss Lucy to say,"You'll have to talk to Mr. Browning about that."

"When he can get that lazy old dog of his to go tree us some more young squirrels I'll fry them up."

"Do you mean 'Old Baccer Worm', Miss Lucy?" Clarence asked.

Bettie swung her left foot and kicked Clarence's leg for asking such a dumb question. She thought they all knew that 'Old Baccer Worm' was long ago dead or had never existed; Bettie wasn't sure which. Clarence let out a howl, jumped back on his chair and leaned over to rub his leg. He shot her a look that said,

"What did you have to do that for?"

"Sorry Clarence," she made the excuse. "My foot slipped off my chair and hit your leg."

"Miss Lucy did you say you might have us a fried apple pie for dessert?"

Bettie knew Miss Lucy's fried apple pie would take Clarence's mind off his hurting leg.

Soon they were all enjoying another piece of fried squirrel with cornbread and brown beans.

After Miss Lucy served them all a fried apple pie and were finished eating Mr. Browning said he would take the bones and the last piece of cornbread out to feed his old dog.

None of them even bothered to ask if 'Old Baccer Worm' was outside to *eat* the scraps. Bettie knew, even if Clarence didn't, that he wasn't outside. But why say any more? If Miss Lucy and Mr. Browning were satisfied with believing he was there, then so be it.

Chapter Twenty Three

1913

The summer Johnny, Clarence, and Bettie were fourteen would be another real turning point in their lives. They didn't know it yet but things would never be the same for them after this summer was over.

This being their second teen year they were no longer in grade school. For the first time since they started school Mrs. Pepperdine wouldn't be their teacher. Over the years they had grown to love Mrs. Pepperdine, *as their teacher*, and they felt the love in return.

But this year they were going to have two teachers; Mrs. Baker and Mr. Wharton, both from Hopkinsville. Johnny nor Clarence looked forward to, nor even wanted to go to high school. But Bettie said they were going and when the time came they did.

Before school started they felt like they should walk to Hopkinsville one more time, maybe even go by Bettie's Aunt Charming Tilley's house for a short visit. That morning Bettie said bye to Belinda and told her she was going for a walk with Johnny and Clarence. Howbeit, she didn't say where and knew her mama wouldn't be looking for her to be back until late afternoon.

The summer before, when they were thirteen, they had started walking to Hopkinsville when they felt bored to death sitting around. One day while sitting around Johnny's house Minnie Rivers first put the idea in their heads.

Maybe it was just in Bettie's head at first because she had to give both Johnny and Clarence a shove to get them started that first time. If Minnie had known what she started she'd probably have felt like Belinda did after she suggested they be forest rangers and go back in the hills looking for a lookout tower.

Last summer's walks to Hopkinsville consisted of the walk there, a drink of water from a pump beside the courthouse, a short rest, and sometimes a swing by Aunt Charming's house before the walk back home. After walking ten miles they were all ready to jump into the creek and cool off. But after that last time they stripped all their clothes off they had all started wearing a pair of shorts under their overalls just for such an occasion. Bettie still didn't think she needed a shirt when she was alone with her friends. When they were out walking she was shirtless just like the boys. But then she wore her bibed overalls that covered part of her front.

It wasn't time yet to pick baccer worms for Mr. Browning, they had helped all three of their mothers plant their gardens and knew of nothing else to do than walk to Hopkinsville.

It was the usual uneventful walk, kicking gravel that was in their way and waving at people as they passed their houses. But at the outskirts of Hopkinsville they were met by a group of men on horseback; all wearing masks to hide their faces.

"Who are you kids, and what are you doing here?" One man barked out to them as if he owned the world.

As usual Bettie started to answer for the boys but Clarence cut her off as if he needed to protect her.

"I'm Bettie...."

"I'm Clarence Clearwater," Clarence cut in. "And these are my friends Johnny Rivers and Bettie Silvercreek."

After Bettie pulled her shirt back on she jumped in to let the man know she wasn't afraid of him, even with his face covered.

"Who are you?" she demanded looking the man squarely in the eyes of his mask.

"You look like a gang of no good thieves."

"What did you do, rob the bank?"

"Oh, a little Miss Priss, ehh." "For your information its none of you'r business who I am."

"But it is my business to know who you are and where you'r from."

They could hear the slur in the man's words and knew he had been drinking beer, or whiskey, maybe moonshine.

"We have just walked from Pembroke," Johnny informed the man.

"All we are doing is going for a walk. We get a drink of water at the courthouse pump and then head back for home."

"Waal, this time you'r gon to head back home without a drink of water," the man growled.

"Now git."

Before we could move another man brought his horse closer to us. "Tell your friend Mr. Browning if he wants to sell his tobacco he best *join* the Dark Tobacco District Planter's Protective Association."

"Join what?" Clarence asked.

"Jes tell him you talked to the Dark Tobacco men, he'll know who we are."

"Now git on back home, whar you belong."

"And don't forget we know who you are and whar you live."

The other man spoke again, "Don't forget to tell Mr. Browning what I said. And you might want to tell him he should be careful when he goes squirrel hunting again too."

By then Bettie was hopping mad; threatening a kind man like Mr. Browning. She would have tore into that man even if he was on a horse but Johnny and Clarence stopped her. They held to her arms and all took a step back from the horse.

"Ok, Johnny said, we'll go home but I'm not telling Mr. Browning anything. If you want him to know something take your mask off and talk to him yourself."

Without looking back they turned then to start home. But they weren't too far away to hear the leader growl,

"Ted, them kids are too smart for their own britches. We'll see to Mr. Browning our self."

"Yeah, Henry, I might just pay him a visit one night after he has his tobacco in the barn."

"Nobody will suspect me since I live in town now. I could probably get away with murder and nobody would ever think of me."

Bettie shot a quick look at Johnny and then Clarence, they knew who those names belonged to. They walked most of the way home hardly speaking to each other; each of them lost in their own thoughts. There were two questions that kept tumbling around in all their minds, who was that gang of men, and why were they stopping people from going into town?

Finally Bettie couldn't be quiet any longer.

"That was Henry Johnson and Ted Brooks talking to us, wasn't it?"

Clarence and Johnny both agreed that they were.

"But how do they know Mr. Browning is our friend?" Clarence asked.

"I dunno," Johnny answered. "But I didn't like the way he threatened Mr. Browning going squirrel hunting."

"Neither did I," Clarence growled. sounding as tough as his fourteen year old voice allowed.

"Henry Johnson is supposed to be a traveling salesman and Ted Brooks is supposed to be too sick to work. How can they be out with a gang of men on horses?"

Those were two more questions they couldn't answer right then, none of them really knew very much about either of the two men on horseback. They walked back to Pembroke that day and went straight to Mr. Browning's house. They found him sitting in the shade whittling and called out their hellos.

"Hello to the Silvercreek gang," he called back.

"What's new," he asked, as if he *expected* them to have something new to tell him.

"Do you know who the Dark Tobacco men are?" Johnny asked.

"We just walked to Hopkinsville," Clarence added. "There was a bunch of men on horseback that stopped us from going into town."

"Do you know who the Dark Tobacco men are?" Bettie asked.

245

"One man said to tell you that you'd better join them if you want to sell your tobacco this year," Johnny told him and went on talking.

"I said I wouldn't tell you but then he threatened you about going squirrel hunting."

"We think we know who the two men are we talked to," Bettie said.

"Do you know who the Dark Tobacco people are?" she asked again.

"Oh, I've been threatened by those men for years. It's first one and then another."

"They think they can force all the tobacco farmers in Kentucky and Tennessee to stop selling their tobacco to the American Tobacco Company and drive the price of tobacco back up."

"They have formed a group called the 'Night Riders,' to scare people."

"When they stopped you kids I guess they forgot it wasn't night any more."

"I wouldn't let them bother you too much."

"Yeah, but they threatened you," Bettie said.

"They might shoot you and make it look like an accident."

"Who did you think you recognized?" Mr. Browning asked as if he didn't already know.

"It was Henry Johnson and Ted Brooks," Clarence spoke first."

"We all knew their names even with masks on their faces."

"Why don't you all set down here and we'll talk about it."

"Miss Lucy, Mr. Browning called, do you have any lemonaid made up? There are three awful thirsty youngsters out here."

Her usual response came back thru the screen door.

"Mr. Browning, you know I have some lemonaid made up but they'll have to come inside and get it."

Then laughter followed as if she were the happiest person in the world to have someone to serve lemonaid to.

They could hear her moving her wheelchair around in the kitchen while she sang to herself.

"Skip, skip, skip to my Lou. Skip, skip, skip to my Lou. Skip, skip, skip to my Lou, skip to my Lou my darling."

A minute later Mr. Browning shooed them toward the back door.

"Go on in," he said. "She's got it ready for you."

When they had their glass of lemonaid from Miss Lucy and thanked her they went back outside to finish talking to Mr. Browning. Johnny carried a second glass for Mr. Browning.

"So you think one of those men might try to shoot me?" Mr. Browning asked in a not too concerned voice.

They all nodded their head, yes, then took a drink of the lemonaid. He went on talking.

"One day when I was walking around the field I felt like someone was watching me."

"Tell you what," Mr. Browning went on. "Lets set us a trap, I think I know which one of these 'J Birds' we'll catch."

"Can you all climb a tree?" He asked them and they all said, "Yes, that they were good tree climbers from looking for the eagle's nest."

"You'll have to be quiet as Indians, too," he said. "Can you do that?"

They didn't know what Mr. Browning had in mind but when he said they had to act like Indians they were all ears. This might be as good as looking for the mysterious keg of silver coins they had buried behind Whispering Pete's house. That was still their secret, even from Mr. Browning.

"Yes," they all assured Mr. Browning, that they could be quiet as any Indian ever born.

"Then in the morning, Mr. Browning began, come by the house and Miss Lucy will have a jar of water for each of you."

"We'll all walk around the field like we are going to pick baccer worms but instead you'll go on into the woods and climb a tree by the path."

"I'll stand around out there like I'm watching and talking to you. You'll have to stay real quiet and wait for someone to walk in on the path to watch me. They won't know but what you are down among the baccer plants."

"What do we do if we see someone," Bettie asked.

"That's the interesting part." Mr. Browning answered her.

"The jar of water you will have won't be for drinking, it will have some of Miss Lucy's red dye in it. And if you are close enough I want you to empty the jars of water on his head."

"That should put a mark on him for a few days."..."We'll know who our spy is," he concluded.

Chapter Twenty Four

By noon time they had stayed quiet so long they could hardly stand it any longer. Bettie's stomach growled from hunger and she was afraid the intruder they were waiting for could hear it. Mr. Browning must have known and tried to get the trap in motion. We heard him give a holler,

"Come on 'Baccer Worm,' lets go get that squirrel."

And sure enough it wasn't long before they heard someone walking toward them on the path in the woods; it was Henry Johnson. He passed by Clarence first, then Bettie and Johnny was last. Being ever so quiet each of them took the jar lids off and were ready to pour the red contents on Mr. Johnson's head.

Mr. Johnson stopped right under Johnny to look at Mr. Browning. It was all the time Johnny needed to pour all the red water he had on Mr. Johnson's head. He let out a holler to rival any

Indian war cry. Mr. Johnson was so startled he started backing up looking up into the trees. Just right, Bettie thought, and poured her jar right in his face. While screaming like a Ban chi and staggering back a few more steps Clarence poured his jar on him too and likewise screamed.

That was all Henry Johnson needed to send him high tailing it back for home. Mission accomplished they walked with Mr. Browning back to the house. They all laughed their heads off while telling Mr. Browning how red Mr. Johnson was.

"He'll wear that for a month trying to get it off," Mr. Browning said. "Just for fun, tomorrow I may go pay him a visit."

They all laughed and talked with Mr. Browning as they walked toward his house. Then they enjoyed one of Miss Lucy's fried apple pies before going home. None of them bothered telling their moms what they had just done.

****

Thru high school their friendship remained intact much as it had thru grade school. But like skinny dipping had abruptly stopped, Bettie pulling her shirt off had also stopped.

Until their senior year Bettie didn't notice Johnny and Clarence were competing for her attention. She had been their pals for so many years it never occurred to her they would ever be anything else. But in their senior year the faculty gave the seniors permission to have a Valentine

Sweet Heart Banquet at the school. The senior's date had to be another student who was presently a junior or senior. Everyone knew Bettie would either go with Johnny or Clarence and wondered which it would be. But just as much they wondered who the other one would be with, if they even came.

After the juniors helped the seniors decorate one of their rooms for the evening, the day for the banquet finally came. All the parents volunteered to bring food and help serve the graduating class.

John and Belinda Latimer, William and Minnie Rivers, George and Maude Clearwater, and Henry Johnson was even home and came with Irma to see his son near graduation.

He'd seen him start and he'd see him finish. He felt proud of Billy for finishing school, something he had been cut short on. All the other parents were there to celebrate their child's graduation from high school, a level of education most of the parents had not achieved.

Right up to the very evening no one in their class knew whether it would be Johnny or Clarence who escorted Bettie to the banquet. Neither one of the boys had planned for another date. Their devotion to each other hadn't gone unnoticed by the faculty or their peers so expectancy of their actions was both uncertain and suspenseful. Even their parents arrived uncertain of what to expect.

When everyone else was there and seated the three empty chairs were obvious to everyone, especially Bettie's parents. By then John and

Belinda couldn't wait any longer, they had left home early to bring food and Bettie was still home then getting dressed for the evening. She had been unwilling to divulge which of the boys was coming to escort her to the banquet but she was planning to be there.

When John and Belinda saw none of the three were there they started to leave the school building anxious about their daughter only to find her seated on the steps between Johnny and Clarence.

"Bettie," Belinda called to her. "Come inside everyone is ready to eat."

The three of them stood then and turned to face her parents.

"I don't know Mama," Bettie answered uncertain about what she wanted to do.

"I was just thinking about skipping the banquet. I couldn't choose one of my friends over the other so we were about to leave."

"Don't be silly, Bettie dear. Come on inside with both escorts don't let that spoil your evening."

So the girls were jealous of Bettie for having two escorts and the boys were jealous of Johnny and Clarence for not ever giving them an opportunity to date Bettie.

One of the prettiest girls in school, so everyone said.

As a wild flower grows, Bettie had blossomed into the most beautiful flower of all.

"She had become one of God's most beautiful flowers," so everyone thought.

The Sweetheart Banquet at Pembroke High School was another of those milestone events that changed the lives of the graduating class. None of the kids really had a sweetheart nor had been allowed to date. If the school had an activity for the kids they went with parents then met with friends. Besides that the boys were too shy to ask a girl for a date and even if they had the girl's parents probably wouldn't have allowed it.

The banquet allowed the young people to choose a partner, just for the evening, and exercise their masculine or feminine wiles against the other. It was an exercise in young adulthood most of the kids enjoyed. However, for Johnny, Clarence and Bettie this was not so, they had interacted with each other for years.

Johnny and Clarence both asked her to be their date but because of their past relationship Bettie couldn't turn either one down. Now here they were, two boys and one girl at a function designed for couples. They all felt awkward, for the first time in her life she wished for just one of them to be special.

Both boys would have done anything possible to gain her favor but neither wanted to push the other away. They were so devoted to Bettie that before a decision was made they consulted her first. They never thought of leaving her out of anything they ever did. About every day they would all be hanging around one of their houses until the *acting* mom shooed the other two back home or all three away from the house.

The banquet was a growing experience for *them* too, different than for others but it helped bring them out of their own little world.

All through school they had been inseparable, not allowing any other boy or girl into their closed circle of friendship. But in three months they would be out of school..., for good.

****

The next ten years had seemed like eternity when they were in the second grade. School wasn't as easy for Johnny and Clarence as it was for Bettie. The boys were ready to quit after their eighth grade was finished, and would have, but Bettie said she was going to high school and they better go too if they ever wanted to talk to her again. When it came time for school to start all three of them were there together ready to start high school without a word of argument or hesitancy from either boy.

Now, it was almost over, what would they do? They were seventeen going on eighteen, what were they to do? They weren't kids any more *dreading* the next school year.

Bettie thought she might like to go to a nursing school in Hopkinsville and become a registered nurse. Clarence and Johnny both knew they didn't want any more school so they would get a job they thought, some place in town, maybe Hopkinsville. There were service stations and restaurants that needed young boys to work.

As circumstances would have it they didn't have to wonder about their future very long. Shortly before their high school graduation President Woodrow Wilson announced on April 6th, 1917 the United States involvement in the European War and called for every able bodied young man to enlist in the Army. Both Johnny and Clarence knew what they would do as soon as school was out.

The boys, who were suddenly young men, turned to Bettie, the one who had held their friendship together for the past twelve years. Going to war held a feeling of uncertainty over them.

"What if one of you doesn't come back? She asked. "What if neither of you come back?"

One day as they talked about their future plans and the looming European War turned worldwide, Johnny blurted out what had been in the back of his and Clarence's minds but never before dared say it.

"Bettie, I love you, will you marry me?"

Before Bettie could even think to answer such a question Clarence said,

"Don't answer him Bettie because I love you too, will you marry me?"

Bettie smiled at each of her beloved friends then placed an arm around Johnny and the other one around Clarence.

"I guess I've known for a long time this day would come but now that it's here I just don't know how to answer. I've *shared my love* with you both for so long I don't know how to choose just one of you."

That evening she was alone with Belinda.

"Mama," she said with a faraway sound in her voice. "How do you know if you love someone?"

"I mean really love someone enough to marry them."

"Why, I don't know!" Belinda stammered. Bettie's unexpected question so surprised her she nearly dropped her knitting needles.

"Do you have anyone in particular in mind?" she asked hoping not.

"Johnny and Clarence, but I don't know which one I love the most. Is it possible to have two husbands?"

Bettie asked the question as if, just in the nick of time, a possible solution to her dilemma had occurred to her.

"No, it isn't possible to have two husbands," Belinda answered her quickly.

"You can get that nonsense out of your head right now. This is one time when you have to make a decision and choose between those two boys."

"Well, how did you decide to marry daddy," she asked.

Belinda looked thoughtful before answering, it seemed such a long time since she had thought about it. She recalled the first time John had stolen a kiss at a church social, she was nineteen. She remembered *tingling* clear down to the bottom of her feet.

"I knew, she finally answered. When he first kissed me. I knew and so will you."

"Have you kissed either of them yet?"

"No, Mama, I haven't kissed them, they are boys."

Bettie said it so strongly Belinda smiled at her honesty and innocence.

"Bettie, I suggest you kiss both of those boys and if you feel anything happen after one of their kisses that you don't feel after the other then you will know..., just like I knew."

Bettie went to bed that night full of anticipation for the next day. She knew she had to see Johnny and Clarence the next day and kiss them. Funny, she thought, all of these years we have run and romped together not one time did either boy ever try to kiss me. Well, tomorrow that was going to change, she was going to kiss both of them good and hard; right on the mouth. If that was the way to determine which one of them she should marry then before tomorrow was over she would know.

Bettie was up early enough the next morning to eat breakfast with her daddy before he left to help with the men who were enlisting every day. Men seemed to be coming from everywhere to enlist in the Army. It was only a matter of time before Johnny, Clarence and nearly every able bodied young man was in the war effort in some way.

But this morning she was up to see her dad off for a special reason. Bettie had gone to sleep thinking about kissing Johnny and Clarence and it was the first thing on her mind that morning. But before she did she wanted to ask her daddy a question.

"Daddy," she began a little embarrassed to ask her own dad what she wanted to know.

"Did you ever kiss anyone besides Mama?"

"Why! Bettie Jean," Belinda exclaimed. "Why on earth would you ask your daddy such a question?"

"Mama, I was just wondering if he felt the same way you did when he first kissed you."

"You know, all tingly feeling."

"Whoa, there young lady," John said. "What was that about your mother feeling all *tingly* when I kissed her? She never told me that."

He gave Belinda a rakish look then moved toward her.

"Maybe we should see if my kiss still makes you feel all tingly."

Taking her in his arms he kissed her, at first just for fun because of what Bettie had said. But Belinda had been the love of his life, so then he kissed her lovingly.

"I'm not a young girl anymore, she said, but I still remember and I still love you too, John."

"Daddy, what did you feel when you first kissed Mama? After your first kiss did you know she was the girl you wanted to marry?"

John had embarrassed all of them but Bettie was eager to know what, if any, reaction he felt during her parents first kiss.

"Did you feel tingly too, like Mama?"

"Do you still get that feeling?"

John could see now Bettie was asking serious questions and wanted answers; he sat back then to face her.

"Bettie, he said trying to find the right words to her questions. Men are different in their emotions than women. I didn't feel all tingly all over like your mother did but when I first kissed her my heart skipped a beat and did a complete flip over itself. I never kissed another girl after that, and yes, I knew she was the one for me."

"But why all the questions about kissing, did you let some boy kiss you?" He asked teasing her.

"**No, Daddy,** she said, I didn't let some boy kiss me but I *have* to kiss Johnny and Clarence today, they both asked me to marry them and I have to know which one is the right one."

John and Belinda gave each other a knowing look and realized maybe for the first time their daughter had grown up. It seemed such a short time ago when they were her age; how had the years slipped by?

Later that morning Bettie ran to each of the boy's houses and told them to be at her house by ten o'clock sharp, "And don't be late," she added.

When they came walking up the road she was waiting, wanting to find out what would happen. Bettie flew out of the front door to wave them around the house and as soon as they were around back she began.

"Johnny, Clarence, both of you asked me to marry you but I didn't know how to say yes to one of you and no to the other one. We have been friends so long I wish I could marry *both* of you but mama said I couldn't do that, I have to choose one of you for a husband."

"Mama said kissing you both was the only way for me to know which one of you I should marry."

"Johnny," Bettie said. "I have decided since you asked me first I should kiss you first, so come on and let's get it over with."

Johnny and Clarence were both flabbergasted at her surprise announcement to them. In all of their years of friendship they had never, even one time, given in to their secret yearnings to be more than her friend. Now, here she was wanting to kiss both of them.

Johnny smiled as he stepped forward to kiss Bettie. It was more than a little *awkward*, for both of them, to bring their mouths together in a kiss. They had bit each other's fingers more than once to break loose during a wrestling match but never before had they put their mouths together.

After a short kiss Bettie pushed away from him.

"*Yuk,*" she said wiping her mouth with the back of her hand. "Your mouth is wet."

"So is yours, Johnny responded, but it tasted good."

"I didn't feel anything, did you?" she asked.

"Nothing but your lips," Johnny replied still smiling at being first.

Bettie wiped her mouth with the back of her hand again, wiping away the kiss; she even spit on the ground.

After a minute more of wiping and spiting away Johnny's kiss Bettie said,

"Ok, Clarence, it's your turn."

Clarence had watched and waited through the first demonstration and now moved quickly, eager to kiss her lips. They embraced, about as natural as a dog kissing a chicken, kissed for a brief moment, then Bettie pushed away disappointed again at what she expected to be her answer.

"*Yuk,*" she said again and wiped her mouth as before, then spit again. "Your mouth is wetter than Johnny's, did you feel anything?" she asked.

"Only your sweet lips," Clarence responded.

"I didn't feel anything from either one of you but your wet mouth, this *isn't* working like mama said it would."

Bettie wiped her mouth again and turned from them in disappointment. She was about to go back inside when Johnny suddenly moved in front of her. Not for a trial kiss or because he had been asked to but because he wanted to kiss her. It was a *loving* kind of kiss, arms gently but firmly around her.

When their mouths came together it wasn't awkward, wet or friend kissing friend. This time Bettie tingled from the top of her head all the way down her body to her feet. She *yielded* to his kiss that could have lasted forever. It left her feeling weak and trembling knowing Johnny was the one.

When he let her go Clarence wanted a second kiss too but she said,

"No, Clarence, it's Johnny, he is the one."

When the boys finally left her they were still friends, but *changed*, again even more.

Bettie went running into the house. "Mama, Mama," she called I love Johnny the most his kiss made me all *tingly* just like you said."

Bettie threw her arms around Belinda and hugged her long and hard.

"I'll always love you Mama, but this is different. I want to *marry* Johnny."

Then just as quick she thought about Clarence, who would love him if she didn't?

Poor Clarence felt like he was all alone now for sure. For the last twelve years their lives had been bonded together like they were encased in a cocoon. Now, he was not only separated from Bettie but from Johnny as well. It never occurred to any of them before but cutting off one member of their gang was like cutting off one of their own fingers. All Clarence knew to do was go home, sit on a porch step and look at the ground.

Chapter Twenty Five

The following week Johnny and Bettie saw each other every day. They hugged each other and Johnny even *stole* a kiss now and then that made her feel tingly every time. Whenever he was with her she felt all giddy and flighty inside. Bettie was a young woman in love for the first time and with one of her best friends.

It wasn't until the end of their senior year of high school that she even thought about loving a boy. And certainly never thought about loving Johnny or Clarence, they were her very best friends.

They were Bettie's friends, pals, protectors, school mates, exclusive club members, but never a boy friend. Neither of them ever came to her mind as a possible candidate for a future husband. Anyway, a husband just wasn't in the cards for Bettie Latimer. Why, she had run with Johnny

Rivers and Clarence Clearwater for so many years, she felt like one of the boys.

Bettie thought about Johnny Rivers' name and then about her own name. After they were married it would be *Bettie Rivers*. Then she thought, what if Clarence had of been the one, her name would be *Bettie Clearwater*. For just a moment her mind went back the first day they went looking for the eagle's nest. Even then both boys had wanted her last name to be their last name too.

But what if I could marry both of them, then it would be Bettie Clearwater Rivers, or Bettie Rivers Clearwater. Maybe even Bettie Latimer, Silvercreek, Clearwater, Rivers. She smiled at the thought and wondered where Clarence was keeping himself, she hadn't seen him since the day she kissed him and Johnny.

She went to his house, as she had done a thousand times before and hollered,

"Clarence, are you inside?" Then went on inside without knocking or waiting for an answer. Maude Clearwater was in the kitchen and stopped only briefly to say,

"Hi, Bettie, where have you been keeping yourself lately, I haven't seen you for at least a week?"

"Didn't Clarence tell you?" she asked.

"Johnny and I are going to be married."

"I would marry both of them but mama said I couldn't have two husbands. She said I had to choose one of them to get married."

"We've been awful good friends. I thought I loved Johnny and Clarence the same but when I kissed them I knew Johnny was the one."

Maude stood listening waiting for her to run down. She always came in talking like she had been wound up and turned on. Maude smiled at her as she listened, trying to hide the disappointment she felt. She wished Clarence had of been the one Bettie chose to marry.

Maude thought Bettie had become the prettiest girl in town with her auburn hair and sparkling brown eyes. The best part about her, she thought, was that Bettie was completely oblivious to the fact that everyone who knew her admired her.

"Goodness, girl, you sure are wound up today. I'm glad you can talk otherwise you might explode. I thought something must have happened with you three kids, I've never seen Clarence look so lost."

"Where is he Mrs. Clearwater, I feel real bad about all of this?"

"He isn't here, he said he was going for a walk, I don't know where."

Bettie guessed where she might find Clarence and told Mrs. Clearwater she would see her again soon. Bettie started for the creek where they had gone many times just to be alone. When she left Clarence's house she began to run, just like she always used to do with Johnny and Clarence on either side of her.

Bettie hadn't wanted to choose one of them over the other, it just all happened so suddenly. She felt an urgency to find Clarence before he..., she couldn't bear the thought of what had just crossed her mind. If she was the cause of Clarence doing something she would never forgive herself.

Reaching the creek Bettie slowed to a fast walk, the crooks in the path didn't afford a hard running pace. She noticed the path didn't look quite as worn as it used to and the weeds were growing out into the path more than ever before.

This was the first time she had gone to the creek that summer and now it was to find Clarence. Their lives had certainly changed over the last three or four years, *they* had changed. She walked quickly, dodging the high weeds and undergrowth to their favorite swimming hole. Bettie didn't see Clarence at first, seated on the ground with his back against the tree trunk where they all stripped their clothes off to go skinny dipping.

Bettie slowed her walk as she rounded the tree and without looking down on Clarence, even for a second, or saying a word, sat down beside him then leaned back against the tree. They sat thus for several minutes before either of them spoke a word. Bettie finally broke the silence.

"I'm sorry Clarence," she began. "I should never have done what I did to you. You have been one of my best friends since we first started school. You were the one that lit into Billy Johnson, when he picked on me in the first grade."

"He would still be picking on me now if it weren't for you and Johnny."

"I'd light into him now if I thought it would make any difference to you," Clarence responded downheartedly.

"Oh, Clarence, Bettie said, I'll always love you too. Loving Johnny doesn't mean I don't love you too. I feel so mixed up about all of this, please don't hate me."

"I think I'd die, she said, if either you or Johnny stopped being my friend."

"In the past I've always had you to talk to when I had a problem," Clarence moaned sorrowfully.

"But it isn't right for me to do that anymore. You chose Johnny instead of me. You two have each other now but I don't have anyone."

His words nearly broke Bettie's heart. She had never seen a more pathetic human being. Here Clarence sat all alone feeling sorry for himself. If she hadn't of been so deeply touched by his words she could have laughed him to scorn. Bettie had done it before and pulled him out of his pity party but they weren't just kids anymore and somehow it didn't seem appropriate now. Instead of laughing she turned to him and held out her hands.

"Come with me, she said, let's walk along the creek and talk."

So, with more coaxing and gentle persuasion Bettie worked her charm on Clarence and soon he was on his feet; she let him pull her up too. They had a long heart to heart talk that day that both settled and brought up issues concerning their friendship and future relationship.

Their friendship was now on more stable ground than it had ever been before. Until that day their friendship had been a shallow, immature friendship. Now, they were adults with adult emotions that were dealt with as adults. From that day forward they both knew they would never marry anyone else.

Bettie allowed Clarence to kiss her and she tingled from the top of her head to the bottom of her feet.

"Oh, no!" She gasped with flushed face.

"Whatever am I to do now," she wailed.

"I *tingled* all over just like when Johnny kissed me. mama said I would know for sure which one of you I should marry when I kissed you; but I don't."

"Oh, don't tell Johnny about this, he'll never understand."

Bettie literally moaned as she thought about her predicament. She wasn't any better off than she had been before this kissing thing started.

Somehow she knew Johnny had to be told, but what, what was she going to tell him? She had already agreed to marry him, maybe even before he enlisted in the Army. Now, if she told him she couldn't marry him,... what might he do?

"Clarence, she moaned, I have to go home, I have to talk to mama."

Bettie left Clarence along the creek and started home. She followed the old path along the creek she had helped keep beaten down. Now there were places where Horse Weeds grew as tall as she was. She had walked the path for years and knew every turn, every rock and every tree root that lay above the ground. She didn't have to think about the path and *wasn't*, her mind was on Johnny and Clarence and what she was going to do about getting married. She had to get home and talk to her mama again, there must be something more about boys than what they had ever talked about.

Bettie had walked possibly a hundred yards from where she left Clarence when suddenly right in front of her stood Billy Johnson.

"Hi, Bettie," Billy said. "Where are you going all alone? It isn't like you to be by the creek without Johnny or Clarence?"

"I'm going home." Unwillingly Bettie answered his question and attempted to pass Billy who stood firmly in the center of the path. Other than the unheard words and smirky looks that no one else saw, this was the first time after seeing Billy in the General Store that he had harassed her.

"What's the hurry," Billy said and moved to block her from getting past.

"Let's go down to the swimming hole and go skinny dipping like you used to do with Johnny and Clarence, Billy sneered. You never invited me but I watched more than once, I knew what you three were doing even if no one else did."

"Get out of the way and let me go past you," Bettie shouted. Her anger was rising at Billy's insolence. The very idea of Billy watching her undress made her burn with anger. She wanted to scratch his eyes out to erase the memory he held of her most private relationship with Johnny and Clarence. She turned to dodge his movement and felt his big hand grip her arm. She struggled to get free from his grasp only to feel his vice like grip tighten on her arm.

"Billy, let go of my arm you are hurting me!" she shouted. But Billy wasn't about to let her go now that he had finally caught her by herself. For years he had watched her run with Johnny and Clarence, always with one or both of them. He had been jealous of them ever since that day at school in the first grade. Picking on her then had been a child's way of getting her attention but his objective was never realized. Bettie only felt scorn for Billy as she watched him bully his way through school.

Clarence came to her rescue that day even though he probably didn't need to. Bettie could out run and out wrestle most boys back then but Billy had always been heavy and stronger than most kids. He saw Billy having an unfair advantage over Bettie and flew into Billy to help even the odds.

Now Billy was pulling Bettie along the path toward the swimming hole. He never relaxed his grip on her arm no matter how hard she pulled back. When they reached the swimming hole she knew Billy intended to make her undress for him.

She couldn't do that, she would rather die first. She had to get free but nothing she did seemed to reach his determined mind.

Like a steam engine, humanly impossible to stop, that doggedly moves a train over miles of track, on he went. On toward the swimming hole he went dragging Bettie kicking and screaming. She was frantic at Billy's irrational behavior when out of nowhere appeared her two knights in shining armor. Billy suddenly stopped dragging her and she heard Johnny say,

"Let her go Billy and then I'll settle with you."

At the very instant Billy released his grip on her arm Clarence hit Billy from behind. He tore into Billy with all of his strength but Billy was bigger and stronger. Johnny was surprised at Clarence's unexpected intervention and stepped aside as they tumbled toward him. Then seeing that Clarence was having trouble with Billy jumped into the fight. Together they wrestled Billy to the ground then beat on him with their fists and rubbed his face against the hard ground. When they stood up Clarence landed the toe of his shoe in the pit of Billy's stomach; for good measure.

When the fight was over Johnny said,

"Billy, if you ever touch Bettie again I'll *kill* you."

"Only if you get to him first otherwise I'll kill him," Clarence added.

As Billy climbed to his feet they each punched him in the ribs one more time. Then together, went to their beloved Bettie and stood with arms around each other while Billy limped away, once again swearing to get even some day.

Chapter Twenty Six

Johnny and Clarence walked on either side of Bettie just as they had all through school. They assured her they would always love her and protect her from men like Billy. It was then that she told Johnny she couldn't marry him and leave Clarence out of her life.

"I love both of you," she said. "I either marry *both* of you or *neither* one."

"As long as you are both alive we'll all remain friends and I'll love each one of you the same."

Bettie settled the issue just as she had on numerous other occasions. Whenever there was a disagreement or dispute between the boys she served as both judge and jury. Her word was final, when she spoke there was no more argument. It wasn't like Bettie was the boss or ring leader of a group, the boys just accepted her decisions when they couldn't seem to make one.

So, on this day they were not surprised at her announcement to them. They were fully aware that the long range effects of this decision could keep them from ever experiencing or knowing the love a man and woman find in marriage. None of them might ever experience fatherhood or motherhood.

Since all three of them were an only child this decision could mean, at their death, all three families would come to an end. No grandparents, no grandchildren. No one would be left to remember them.

Bettie didn't tell Belinda about the incident with Billy Johnson. Somehow, by not talking about it she hoped she could forget it, that it would go away. Johnny and Clarence knew about it and that was enough. For the next several days one or both of them was at her house acting as a sentinel on duty. They had seen what Billy tried to do and didn't want it to happen again.

The only problem was they knew it wasn't going to be very long before they enlisted in the Army, then who would watch out for her. As kids their close knit threesome had been great but already they were running into trouble keeping their group together as adults.

They never spoke a word to Belinda about Billy Johnson or their marriage decision. But Belinda had watched those three for the last twelve years and could pretty well read their actions. When there was something going on they didn't want to talk about she couldn't get more than three words out of either of them. When they went in that day they barely said hi to her then went on to the backyard where they stayed until Johnny and Clarence left to go home.

Some days Belinda felt like she had three kids to take care of and feed. A lot of the summer days she fixed them all lunch but if the boys were still there at supper time she sent them away with one word, "Home."

"You boys need to go find out where your real mama and daddy call home."

She noticed that Clarence stopped coming by after Bettie announced she loved Johnny the most. But now, here he was again without any explanation or noticeable change in behavior. They passed through the house single file with barely an acknowledgment she was there.

Many times before Belinda had seen how devoted the boys were to Bettie so when they both started showing up again everyday she knew something had happened. She also noticed that Bettie stopped talking about getting married. One day as Belinda looked out of her back window on them she said to herself,

"Lord, what am I going to do with that girl when the boys leave home, she doesn't have one other close friend?" "Not one single girl friend."

As the school year came to a close and graduation drew near John and Belinda talked to Johnny and Clarence's parents about getting together for one big party.

"The boys are going to be leaving soon," John said to their parents.

"Bettie would like to do something special for them before that time."

The Clearwater and Rivers' families both agreed that it would be a good time for them to all get together for their birthdays.

"I know Johnny would like a party, he dearly loves homemade ice cream," Minnie Rivers said.

"And Clarence too," Maude Clearwater put in. "I'll have some fresh strawberries by then to put in the ice cream; that is Clarence's favorite kind."

So the party date was set and plans were made to make this birthday party a memorable occasion. This party wasn't to be a couple's party as the Sweetheart Banquet had been so the three young people wouldn't feel out of place together. John teasingly asked Belinda if she minded him asking another lady friend to sit with them.

"Just to even things out," he teased.

"The day I share you with another woman I will be six feet underground," she said so firmly that John didn't think it wise to continue his tease.

When the day came for the party Belinda baked a huge birthday cake for all three families. Everyone met at the *Latimer house. Or Silvercreek house*. That was an old subject none of them thought about any more. They had long since stopped talking about finding the keg of silver coins. Johnny, Clarence and Bettie were the only ones to ever know the secret of the silver coins.

George and Maude Clearwater arrived and brought their ice cream freezer.

"I have a big chunk of ice in the cart, George said. I stopped at the ice house in town so we would have plenty. I think I could eat a freezer full myself."

"I picked strawberries this morning, William Rivers added. Minnie has them all cut up ready to put in the ice cream. I think I could eat a freezer of ice cream too. I'm glad we brought our freezer along or these kids might not get any."

John greeted the visitors then joined in with the other two men's good natured banter.

"It sounds like I better get our freezer out too. I intend to eat all of the ice cream I want and that will be most of a freezer."

The joking and laughter among the parents was an effort to make everyone forget what this birthday party really meant. They were all proud of their kids, as parents usually are. As far as they were concerned there weren't three other young people in Pembroke that could match theirs. They had watched them grow up together, go to school together and play together. Clarence, Johnny and Bettie were like brothers and sister that had three sets of parents.

"I say we let the young people turn the freezers, George said heartily, a little pay back for all the things they have put us through."

"George, you ought to be ashamed of yourself making those kids freeze their own ice cream,"

Maude said. "Anyway, you men don't know the half of what these kids have caused us women to worry about."

"Now, Maude, don't blow a gasket I was only joking," George replied.

The parents all laughed at the two because Maude was always ready to call George down over some ridiculous thing he said or did. And George did it just to rile her. He would go on telling the most preposterous tale until he saw Maude's face getting red and he would know he had gotten to her. She'd come back with, "Now George, you know that's a lie."

"If I'm lying, I'm dying," George would say.

And so on and so on they would go until George finally gave in to, maybe *stretching the truth* just a little bit.

"They are a pair," John had told Belinda several times.

"Maude knows when George is serious and when he is stretching the truth. But I think she enjoys it just as much as he does."

The women prepared the ice cream adding their own little touch to the recipe then called for their children to come take it to the freezers.

George had the chunk of ice in burlap bags and hauled it out on the ground where he broke it up with a sledge hammer. When the freezers were filled with ice and salted down, Clarence, Johnny and Bettie began turning the handles. The men sat back down under a shade tree and picked up their conversation again.

"Those men are sitting out there telling lies while the kids turn the freezers," Maude fumed.

"They are all right," Belinda assured her.

"If anyone needs help it will be Bettie and her dad has his eye on her. Anyway, this gives them something to do together."

No one had said it but, especially the mothers knew what it would mean for their children when they were soon separated. Belinda knew it would be as hard on Bettie staying home as it would be on Johnny and Clarence leaving. They would all be separated for the first time since they started school. She feared for the boy's life going off to war but she wondered what Bettie's life would be like while they were gone.

Then a real fear griped Belinda's heart, one that she hadn't seriously considered before. What if something happened to Bettie, the unexpected accident, the illness that could take her life the same as a bullet could take the life of Johnny or Clarence. The future was so uncertain for young people these days, not like it had been when she was growing up. She prayed earnestly, *"Lord, protect these three young people's lives, only You know what lies ahead for them."*

Belinda's musings were brought back to the present when she heard talking.

"I think the freezers are getting cold," Minnie said. "Maybe we should see if the ice cream is frozen."

They took spoons and bowls out with them to be prepared if the ice cream was ready to eat. They knew the men were waiting more impatient than the kids. The ice cream *was* ready and the men were called to get a bowl, then when they were all together John reviewed the three young people's lives in a serious tone Bettie would never forget.

"Before we enjoy the ice cream and cake you ladies have made I want to take time to thank God for it. But for much more than something that will give us temporary satisfaction to our appetite,.. our kids."

"We have all watched them through the various stages of adolescence as they were becoming young men and women. They are no longer becoming but have now reached that point in their lives. It has been an absolute joy to me, as I'm sure it has been to each of you other parents, to watch them grow, mature and become what they are today."

"Johnny and Clarence, I wish you God speed with journey mercies until you are back home." He finished talking to the boys and turned to Bettie.

"Bettie, whatever else you might do let me give you one word, *wait*." "Don't rush to get your life ahead of God, just wait."

"Now Lord, we commend Johnny, Clarence and Bettie into Your hands We ask You to watch over *them, protect them, and bring them all back together someday. Amen."*

As John finished he looked around and saw almost everyone was close to tears.

"Belinda, why don't you ladies serve the honored guests first? Fill up their bowls and give them all they want. You ladies go next and take all you want, then if there is any left us older men will clean it up."

"I know your tricks John Latimer," Belinda came back. "I haven't lived with you for twenty years and not learned your tricks."

"You make it sound like you are only getting the left over's but you are hoping there will be half a freezer of ice cream left for each of you men to clean up."

His plan worked too, soon huge bowls overflowing with ice cream and luscious strawberries were being carried away to a place where its savory goodness could be enjoyed. Everyone, even the men, had all of the homemade ice cream they could eat. It was a day each member of the party would hold in their memory, a day never to be *repeated* but never *forgotten*.

In just a few days Clarence and Johnny enlisted in the Army. Major John Latimer was there to help process the men that day and saw them off. At the same time he received new orders and within a week he was gone too.

Their life had been running, paling and playing together from the time they started school until Johnny and Clarence enlisted in the Army. But before the boys left they made one last trip down to the bank of their swimming hole to retrieve their silver dollars. Each of them took one of the dollar coins Whispering Pete gave them and held it in their hand;remembering. In an unexpected motion Johnny spit on his wrist and held it out. After Clarence followed suit and placed his on Johnny's, they looked at Bettie. Without a second's thought she spit on her wrist and then they all rubbed them together just like they did when they were six years old. The boy's sudden absence would leave her without friends and the protection of her strong arm buddies that were always close by.

Up until then their lives had been simple but at eighteen the world looked upon them as adults. The Army was taking two young boys and would turn them into soldiers that might come back maimed and scarred for life.

Everyone's main concern was for the young men being sent into war but, being left alone, Bettie could be easily picked *as a wild flower*. A tragedy could be waiting for her; lurking around the next corner. A tragedy that would leave her life as maimed and scarred as the boys when they came home from the War.

The Latimer women were really alone now, not a man or even a boy was in the house as there had always been before Major Latimer was sent away. Belinda missed John but this had been her life ever since they were first married twenty years ago. This was Bettie's first experience at being alone, *really alone*. She didn't have one other close friend than Johnny and Clarence.

For the last twelve years Johnny and Clarence had been Bettie's whole life; and now they were gone. After they enlisted in the Army she moped around the house for a week looking for something to do. Belinda could hardly tolerate her actions any longer. It was then that Belinda thought, maybe, she had an idea that would help Bettie.

If only she could have known. Before they left Johnny or Clarence had always been around. Belinda never thought about Bettie's wanderings being unsafe. But now...

Chapter Twenty Seven

When Johnny and Clarence enlisted in the Army Bettie was as *lonesome* as lonesome could get. After they were gone she moped around in the house like she didn't have a friend in the world. John had already been sent to Europe and Belinda couldn't stand to see Bettie in such turmoil. One day she had an idea she hoped would draw her out of her depression.

"Why don't you go into Hopkinsville, watch a movie and stay overnight at your Aunt Charming's house. I hear your Uncle George hasn't left for the war yet, you could talk to him."

Reluctantly and with only a smidgen of interest Bettie agreed to Belinda's idea. Bettie always enjoyed staying over night at her Aunt

Charming and Uncle George's house but this time she'd rather have stayed home with her mama.

"Mama," she said still looking for an excuse to stay home. "Maybe we could bake some Oatmeal cookies. That sounds good?"

Belinda smiled at her as she always did but she knew it would do Bettie more good to get out of the house. Belinda knew Bettie wouldn't stop asking to bake cookies until she said yes. Maybe Bettie would feel better, Belinda knew she would feel better just getting Bettie out of the house.

"Oh, all right," Bettie said. "Maybe I'll see someone in town to talk to," She responded with little enthusiasm but agreed to let her mama drive her into Hopkinsville that evening.

At the theater Bettie joined Sadie Plummer and Jackie Brooks who had also been chased out of the house. It seemed there was nothing for the girls to do now that they were out of school. They weren't school kids anymore knowing the next school year would be starting before they were ready. But just the same before this summer they'd always known what they would soon be doing.

It seemed to them that the boys got to do everything. If they wanted to leave home and get a job, that was ok. But if one of the girls wanted to leave home, they were too young and still needed parental supervision.

When the War started all the men, and boys out of school, were joining the Army in droves and sailing away to Europe or Africa. Some place far away from home where the girls would never get to go. The most exciting thing they could do was make something from home and send to a husband or sweetheart.

****

Johnny and Clarence were green kids when they left home at eighteen; about as *green* as green gets. All their exploring the woods around Pembroke and looking up and down Silvercreek for the keg of silver coins didn't prepare them for the Army. But after six weeks of basic training at Camp Campbell and then being sent directly overseas, they weren't so green any more.

When they stepped off the bus from Hopkinsville at Camp Campbell they were met by a drill Sergeant with a voice, years later they said, sounded like a bullhorn. Everything he said, he shouted. Johnny almost got them in trouble when he whispered to Clarence.

"I wonder if he has a volume button."

"I heard that," he shouted. "Who's brave enough to say it to my face?" When no one stepped forward he smirked,

"Just as I thought, a bunch of sissys."

"Just so you remember who is in charge here, all of you drop down and give me 50 push-ups."

That night when the lights were out and the door closed he apologized to the other men. After that day Johnny made sure the Sergeant didn't hear him when he grumbled.

When the Sergeant told them where to go, he shouted. When he told them what to do, he shouted. When they were told to get up, he shouted. When they were told to go bed, he shouted.

He told them,

"If you don't know who to salute then salute everyone that has something on their uniform different than yours."

He barked out orders from five o'clock in the morning until they were told lights out at eight o'clock that night. Six days a week, the only rest they had was on Sunday. They were told they could attend a church service Sunday morning but all anyone wanted to do was rest and sleep.

The boys wanted to write home to their mom and dad but mostly they wanted to talk to Bettie. For some unexplainable reason they *both* had the feeling that Bettie needed them.

"I can't shake the feeling about Bettie," Clarence finally said.

Johnny said, "Yeah, I feel the same way." "If there was a way to get out of here we'd head for home."

Clarence agreed, "But there isn't a way out, a guard stands at the gate day and night to make sure none of us leave."

The first two Sundays they were so dog tired, like most of the other new men, they slept in most of the day. Late in the afternoon they dragged their tired bodies out of bed in time to get cleaned up and to the mess hall for the supper meal.

Finally, by the third Sunday they were beginning to feel like they would live thru their basic training. That afternoon they both wrote a letter to Bettie, a first for them writing anyone a letter. As they sat with pencil and paper Clarence was first to ask,

"What do you say first in a letter, Dear Bettie, Hi Bettie, or just Bettie?"

"I dunno," Johnny gave his usual response. "But I think I'll say Hi Bettie. Her mom used to call her Bettie dear so I don't think we should call her dear Bettie."

Clarence thought that over and decided Johnny was right, they weren't writing love letters so Hi Bettie sounded right. After a few more minutes of thought he said,

"But what comes after that?"

"I dunno," Johnny responded again I never wrote a letter before either."

"What do *you* want to tell her?" Clarence asked.

"I dunno, but I have an idea. Instead of us both writing the same thing why don't you ask her what she has been doing and I'll tell her what we have been doing."

Most of the afternoon they labored over their letters, it was the most grueling Sunday afternoon they could remember. When the three of them had been together it was never hard to tell each other their secrets or ask each other questions. Their mouth opened and out it came.

"Why is it so hard to write down on paper what's going thru our heads?" Clarence moaned.

Suddenly an idea popped into Johnny's head when he remembered he couldn't tell Bettie anything about Camp Campbell because it was classified. He didn't know if he knew any classified information but he didn't want to chance getting in trouble if he did.

"Clarence, I don't want to get us in trouble with the Army, I better just stick to telling Bettie the simple stuff."

"I'll say, It's real nice here, the new men have a building all to our selves."

"Each one of the men has his own bed."

"We have a real nice man training us to be good soldiers, he takes us on long walks to let us get plenty of exercise."

"They give us three good meals every day."

"And this nice man wakes us up every morning so we won't be late for breakfast and turns the light out every night so no one has to get out of bed to go to the light switch."

"We will hate to leave Camp Campbell but word is after six weeks we will all be sent someplace. We might not be together then but we hope so."

They didn't know yet but they, along with hundreds of other new men, would be sent directly to Fort Knox, Kentucky to become a part of the 3rd Infantry Division.

Bettie's return letter reached them only days before deployment from Camp Campbell leaving them no opportunity to write another letter. They were gone and she didn't even know when.

The Army not only pull them away from home and Bettie but after their basic training was over they were sent to different overseas bases. Both were sent out in the 3rd Infantry Division but Johnny was assigned to an outfit going to North Africa while Clarence, along with hundreds more, were given new orders to join up with the 53rd Infantry in Germany.

****

The movie was only a short reprieve from the doldrums the girls all felt. After the movie Bettie said good bye to Sadie and Jackie then walked to her Aunt Charming and Uncle George's house. Aunt Charming was always fun to stay over night with and hoped she could lift her spirits. Bettie was disappointed to find she was gone to Louisville and only Uncle George was home. She soon said good night to him and trudged upstairs to the bedroom that always awaited her.

After breakfast the next morning Bettie asked her Uncle George Tilley to drive her back to Pembroke. She had walked it many times with Johnny and Clarence but the way she was dragging around she would have been all day getting home.

When they reached Pembroke Bettie asked him to let me out near the grocery store.

"I want to go for a walk," she told him. "Just to be alone."

Bettie knew where she wanted to go, down to the creek by the old swimming hole where she had gone so many times with Johnny and Clarence. But walking from the grocery store to the creek took her on a different route than going from home. Without *thinking*, or *caring*, where her walk took her she went by the one place she shouldn't have gone; Billy Johnson's house.

All she wanted was to visit the special place of her childhood where she could feel the presence of her two best and only friends. As she walked the path, eyes down cast, she could hear Johnny say, "Want to jump in the creek and cool off?"

Clarence would try and fool him by saying, "Naw, not today," and then suddenly take off running. But Johnny knew, and Bettie soon learned his trick too; they would both be ready to run.

Bettie could out run both of them but down the path they all ran, pell mell, stumbling, laughing, trying to get ahead of each other, stomping the life out of any green grass or weed trying to grow into their pathway. They kept that dirt path clean of any over growth and would be half undressed by the time they reached the swimming hole.

"The last one in is a rotten egg," she'd say and off went the last of their clothes.

This was the first time since they started school she was unprotected, vulnerable to the one who for twelve years had sworn *vengeance*. Bettie had no idea Billy would be waiting for her or that he *ever* meant her any real harm. It had started when they were just kids and she grew up thinking Billy was no different than any other bully kid she encountered. Bettie just always knew she didn't want him to touch me.

With downcast eyes she wasn't aware Billy had seen her coming and guessed where she was going. More than once he had *watched* the three loners strip their clothes off and jump in the water. He had wanted to join them but knew they wouldn't stay if he did; so he watched. Finally, Bettie was alone and Billy knew Johnny and Clarence wouldn't be coming to her rescue. They were gone, finally gone out of his way. Where ever the Army had sent them, they were gone.

During their high school years Billy Johnson had caused his share of trouble; and then some. After Mrs. Pepperdine had long endured Billy's troublesome ways he thought he could continue to push his teachers to the limit without undergoing any backlash. But when Bettie Latimer, Sadie Plummer, Jackie Brooks, Johnny Rivers and Clarence Clearwater graduated from high school, Billy didn't. To graduate he was allowed one more year to make up all the work he had failed to do.

He was still home while Johnny and Clarence enlisted in the Army. Billy was home to settle matters with Bettie while her friends were gone to fight in a European War they might not come home from. The only people that really mattered to her were gone and might not return. With her only friends gone she thought her whole life was turned upside down but she soon found out, quicker than she ever imagined, the next moments would change her life forever.

It just so happened Billy's dad was making one of his infrequent visits home for Irma to wash and iron his clothes. She was busy at work when Billy come rushing in to his dad. She couldn't hear what Billy whispered to him but watched as they both hurried from the house. She feared she didn't want to know and tried to forget the incident.

Billy led his dad, *wasn't that rich*, a son leading his dad to commit the kind of violent act he had been told to do when necessary to get what he wanted. On the way out of the house they grabbed three paper bags then rushed to get ahead of Bettie. They punched two holes in two of the bags to see thru and then pulled them over their heads; the other one was for her. They hid in tall weeds along the path while they waited for her to come by.

As Billy waited for her to come by his only thought was to gain the vengeance he had waited and longed for; with no thought of what he was going to do to her life. No thought that in a moment of self-gratification he would ruin her life. His heart was pounding, he had never committed such a hateful, yet satisfying, act before. When Billy reached out and dragged her into the weeds his dad slipped the extra bag over her head.

Bettie never saw their faces but afterward she remembered it was the same strong hand that had first pulled on her at school, and then dragged her along the creek one day as the one that dragged her into the weeds. Each one of the assailants held Bettie down while the other *forced* himself on her.

Everyone in town had said,

"Bettie was a beautiful child, the wild flower of Pembroke, Kentucky had blossomed."

Now, Billy thought, she was ready to be picked...and all alone.

The *foul deed* was done, the vengeance against Johnny and Clarence was *satisfied.* Her *life* was ruined but neither Billy nor his dad felt any remorse for their actions. On their way home Billy's dad slapped him on the back.

"You are a *man* now, son."

Billy smiled satisfaction in hearing his dad's words of approval. Finally, Billy knew vengeance was his and neither Johnny or Clarence was there to protect Bettie...to stop him.

Later that afternoon when she found the courage to go home Belinda sensed something was wrong. Bettie was more withdrawn than before going into town. She scarcely answered her mama's questions while sitting with her head down in embarrassment, shame.

"Did you see a nice movie?" Belinda asked.

"Yes, Mama," was all she could say.

"Did you see any of your old school friends while in town?"

"Yes, Mama," again was her only reply.
"Did you talk to your Uncle George?"
"Yes, Mama," was her struggled reply.

Finally Belinda gave up and told Bettie to go on upstairs, get washed and then have a nice rest. Bettie ran water in the tub as hot as she could stand getting into then scrubbed herself trying to feel clean but knew she'd never be clean again.

Afterward she went to her room where she stayed for the next week only coming out to eat and go to the bathroom. Belinda could see the *shame* Bettie tried to keep hidden that day and throughout the following week. When Bettie left her room and tried not to face her mama, Belinda had a sinking suspicion she knew why.

Belinda could see Bettie was not fully recovering from that terrible experience, whatever it had been. But gradually she began to come out of the shell she had placed around herself. Bettie never told Belinda what happened to her while returning from town that day but she thought she figured it out.

Belinda wrote a letter to her sister, Charming, and ask if she knew what had happened to Bettie only to find out Charming hadn't been at home the day Bettie was there. Belinda's heart stopped beating. She didn't tell Charming what she suspected about her husband. Bettie hadn't said as much and Uncle George Tilley had just left for North Africa.

If only Clarence or Johnny had known what Billy Johnson did to Bettie they would have gotten home somehow. They wouldn't have cared what the Army did to them they would have run off from Camp Campbell to get home.

Bettie knew if they *ever* knew what Billy had done they would kill him for sure, just like they said. She didn't want that and couldn't ever chance letting them know. But, anyway they were gone and Bettie couldn't get to them nor they to her. She felt a great gulf between them for the first time since they started school.

All thru school Bettie had Johnny and Clarence at her side; no matter what. It didn't matter how she felt or how bad her attitude was, Johnny and Clarence were always her true-blue friends. She yearned for their company more than she ever had before. She really needed them; but they could never know.

Bettie thought about leaving home to find them but she didn't know where to go. She knew they went to Camp Campbell but even if she went there she wouldn't be allowed on base to see them. For days after Billy's attack she stayed in her room and cried. Bettie didn't want to talk to anybody, not even her mama.

Eventually life for her and Belinda went back to as near normal as it would ever be again. However, two months later Bettie knew she had to tell her mama about that day. She didn't know how since she'd never talked to Belinda of such things.

Finally, one day Bettie went to where Belinda was sitting and sat beside her. She didn't say anything at first, just sat with head down.

"Mama I think I'm...,"

"*Don't say it*," Belinda interrupted her.

"I don't ever want to hear you say the awful thing that has happened to you. We will go away where nobody knows us and *'I'* will have a *'new'* baby when we come home."

Belinda began telling everyone she saw that they were going to take an extended trip to Topeka, Kansas; and maybe stay a few months visiting her mom and dad. But they didn't really go to Topeka, they went to Nashville, Tennessee where they stayed until Bettie's baby was born.

"I will tell your father it was *Johnny Rivers* that did this to you, we will never tell a soul what really happened."

And they didn't. There was no authority in Pembroke to report it to, no one to do anything that would help, what was done was done; so Bettie kept quiet.

Nine months after that horrible day walking home her baby girl, she named Delores, was born. Delores was the prettiest little baby she had ever seen; with auburn hair just like her mama, Grandma Belinda, and Great Grandma Henshaw.

Bettie never told Belinda that she was certain Billy was the one; Belinda never asked and Bettie never told her. And, Bettie never wanted even her mama to know Billy Johnson was Delores' father.

As far as Bettie was concerned Delores didn't have a father, he was already dead.

In the worst way Bettie wanted to be her babies mama.; She wanted to hold her and love her as a mother should but Belinda wouldn't have it that way.

"No, she said, I have to be Delores's mother."

And that's the way it was when they went home. All anyone, including Johnny and Clarence, ever knew was that Belinda had a new baby. As everyone else, they were told Bettie had a new baby sister.

Chapter Twenty Eight

Bettie wasn't a *little* girl any more running with her two best and only friends, Johnny and Clarence. They were long gone and Bettie was a mother, or a big sister, or something. She didn't know what she was anymore. Belinda said she had to pretend to be Delores's mama so no one would ever know about what happened to Bettie.

Bettie wondered who she had to be protected from now, and why. It wasn't her that had done the wrong. She wanted to walk all over town carrying a big sign telling everyone what Billy had done to her.

She watched Belinda change Delores's diaper, feed her, hold her, rock her and sing the songs to her she had sung to Bettie when she was a little girl. She could hardly stand to watch her mama and not be able to hold her own little baby.

It tormented Bettie day and night until she was in a worse mess than she'd been the day it all started. She spent days in her room all alone, sometimes walking the floor and then she'd flop down on her bed and cry. For hours she'd cry until there wasn't another drop of moisture left that could run from her eyes.

After a couple of months back home watching Belinda take care of her baby she couldn't stand it any longer and knew she had to get out of the house or go crazy.

"Mama, she said, I'm going to Hopkinsville and get a job. I don't know if I'll be back but I can't stand it here any longer."

"Oh, please Bettie dear, don't go. I know it's hard for you but its hard for me too. I'm not as young as I was when you were a baby. And all of this pretending isn't going to stop, its only getting started."

"What do our friends think about Delores?"

"Do they think I'm really Delores's mother?"

"Do you *really* believe people in Pembroke think we went away just when I was about to have a baby?"

"And what about *Delores's* father?"

"Don't you think he might guess who Dolores is?"

"What am I supposed to say when he comes asking questions?" "And your own daddy, Bettie." "What about him?"

Tears ran from Belinda's eyes like Bettie never saw before. Bettie didn't know what to say to her but somehow she wanted to be a little girl again. Running in and out of the house with Johnny and Clarence to get one of her mama's fresh oatmeal cookies. Bettie wanted her mama to hug her in the worst way; instead of Delores.

It was the only time Bettie ever heard Belinda talk about such things. Belinda had always been Mama to Bettie, as well as Johnny and Clarence. It never occurred to her that Belinda was being effected in such a *dreadful* way. Up until now it seemed like Belinda had always been a mama; as well as all the other mamas she knew.

"I'm sorry Mama," Bettie said. "But I just have to go, I can't stand it any longer; being here and not permitted to be my babies mama."

She was a grown woman now, not a kid running with Johnny and Clarence. But Bettie struck out that day walking to Hopkinsville. When folks saw her walking the road alone they wondered why her friends weren't with her. More than one lady waved to her as she walked by their house. When she walked that road with Johnny and Clarence it didn't seem far at all but walking it alone made her feel like she'd never get there. And it was freezing cold too.

Bettie had no idea where she was going or what she could do when she reached Hopkinsville, she just wanted a job. The first thing that caught her eye was the Princess Cafe so she went inside and told the lady she *needed* a job.

"What's your name, *honey*?" The lady asked.

"Bettie Latimer," she told her without even thinking of telling her it was Bettie Silvercreek. Surprising what a couple of years and maturity does to a person's mind.

"Folks just call me *Princess*," she responded.

"How old are you, honey?" Princess asked ignoring her name and Bettie wondered why she even bothered to ask.

"Eighteen," she said. Bettie wondered what her next question would be so she didn't tell her anymore information than she had asked for.

"Why do you need a job, honey." Princess asked while looking Bettie up and down as if she were going to buy her.

Bettie wasn't sure that she liked being looked at as if she were a prize calf in the county fair. And she hadn't thought about being asked that particular question.

"I, I don't know," she stammered.

"I just do."

"Well, if you don't know *why* you need a job then I don't guess I have one for you."

"Do you mean that you would give me a job if I told you why I need it?"

"That about sums it up, honey."

Bettie wished Princess would stop calling her honey and tried to think of a quick reason for needing a job.

When nothing else came to her mind she blurted, "My mama's at home with a new baby and I need to work." That wasn't a lie, well maybe some of it but she thought God would forgive her; given the situation.

Princess seemed to be impressed with that answer but then she asked,

"Where do you live?"

"Pembroke," Bettie said and knew right away that wasn't good.

"How you going to get from Pembroke to the Princess Cafe every day, walk?"

Before Bettie could answer Princess's first question Princess said, "You're walking right now, aren't you honey?"

Bettie said, "Yes, she was walking and didn't know how she could get to work every day, but she'd try." She answered the question quickly before Princess said no to a job.

"I tell you what, honey. You are a pretty girl, a very pretty girl, I think *you* would be good for business."

"There just so happens to be a room in back of the cafe, I sometimes use it but you can use it temporarily until you get your own place to stay."

"Of course I take half of everything you make in the back room," Princess added.

"What do you mean, make in the back room?" "I'll be working out here with you all the time..., won't I?"

Princess gave her another appraising look up and down that made her uncomfortable.

"We'll see, honey, we'll see," she said.

"Come on back here and get an apron on so you'll look like you're working. I'll show you around and then if anyone comes in I'll show you how to wait on them."

The afternoon passed slowly but business picked up toward evening. People started coming in for their evening meal and before long Bettie was taking orders without Princess' help. Only one man made an unkind remark to her but that was to be expected Princess told her.

"Most people who come in here act like we are all family but ever once in a while we get a real jerk."

"Seeing as how you are new and so pretty, did any of the men ask you to take them to the back room?"

"No," Bettie told Princess and gave her a questioning look but Princess asked nothing more.

Princess had a peculiar glint in her eye when she asked Bettie about the back room and Bettie couldn't imagine why anyone would want her to take them to the back room. Anyway, Princess had said she could use it to sleep in until she found her own room.

They closed the cafe for the night and Princess locked the door behind her. Bettie went to the back room and fell into bed; exhausted, the day had been long. She didn't want to think about her mama, Delores, or home. All she thought about before drifting off in a worn out sleep was Johnny and Clarence.

"Where are they?" "Are they ok?" Her last thoughts were of her two best and only friends, then sleep enclosed her.

Bettie couldn't believe it was time to get up when she heard Princess rattling and banging pans. It was hardly daylight.

"Have you been to bed?" she asked.

"Honey, when you get to be my age sleep seems to belong to someone else. So I get up and come to the cafe, there are always a few hungry men come in for breakfast."

"Why don't you go get yourself fixed up real pretty for the men and then come help me."

There it was again, Princess telling her she was pretty and the day had just started. Bettie could see already it was going to be an awfully long day. And it was, by afternoon she could hardly stay on her feet. She guessed Princess could see she was about to drop and told her to go get some rest before the evening rush started.

Bettie dropped off immediately and it was five o'clock when Princess woke her.

"Honey, she said, wake up there is a man asking to come back here and see you."

Then it struck her like lightening, she was being so gullible, so naive. Princess gave her a job only because she was pretty and she thought a pretty young girl like herself would bring in all the single men in town. "Stupid me," she thought.

"These men aren't coming just to eat but for me to take them to the back room; that's where she made money the easy way. Well, she'd had enough of the Princess Cafe and told Princess to pay her for the day; she was thru.

Princess paid her two dollars and Bettie had been given fifty cents in tips. Bettie picked up her things and immediately started back for Pembroke. It was a long walk and it was cold. She was never so glad to see home until she started thinking about her baby again and knew she couldn't stay.

Just as Belinda always had, Bettie's mama was waiting to find out where Bettie had been. Belinda hugged her and Bettie could see her worried look.

"Hi, Mama," she said. "I worked in Hopkinsville at the Princess Cafe but I couldn't stay there and do what Princess wanted me to do."

Bettie looked at *her* baby again and knew it was true, she couldn't stay here either, it hurt too much.

"Mama, do you have enough money to buy me a bus ticket to Elizabethtown?"

"That's near Fort Knox where Johnny and Clarence were probably sent from Camp Campbell. When they come home they might come there before coming here; maybe I can see them there when they come home."

Belinda looked at Bettie and knew she was running away. For the last twelve years she'd been running with Johnny and Clarence that led to this moment. Now she was running away for good; because she couldn't raise Delores as her own baby. Belinda didn't argue or try to persuade her to stay at home any longer. Instead she went to her purse and returned with money.

"Bettie dear, I've been saving this ten dollars for a long time, it must have been for you."

Belinda's eyes were heavy laden with tears as she hugged Bettie that day knowing this time Bettie wouldn't be back.

"You'll always be my little girl Bettie, and I'll love Delores just as I've always loved you."

They hugged not wanting the embrace to end. Bettie left home that day knowing she wouldn't be back. She looked in the direction of Silvercreek and thought of the secrets it held. The secrets with Johnny and Clarence, the keg of silver hid behind Whispering Pete's house, Mr. Browning and Miss Lucy. The question Ole Moses Gray asked them years ago, "Do you know the Lawd, and does the Lawd know you," was still a mystery to her.

But most of all the *secret* only she knew, and would *ever* know, was who Delores's father was.

Note from the Author.

Bettie's story is a work of fiction and every word, action, and thought is expressly of the author. The towns of Pembroke, Hopkinsville, and Elizabethtown, Kentucky and the military installations of Camp Campbell, (now Fort Campbell) and Fort Knox, Kentucky are authentic. However, neither installation existed at the time my story began. Fort Knox began in 1905, Camp Campbell in 1942.

Gray Gates Strawberry Farm was a real farm that existed then. As early as 1905 Pembroke hosted an annual horse show that drew wealthy people such as the Vanderbilts. The Ackerman House Hostelry accommodated some of the guests.

Kentucky is well known for Mammoth Cave and Horse Cave as well as many other lesser known caves but the one in this story is fictional.

The words of the negro spirituals are copied and authentic. Also this explanation of their origin is copied for authenticity.

"The lyrics of negro spirituals were tightly linked with the lives of their authors: slaves. While work songs dealt only with their daily life, spirituals were inspired by the message of Jesus Christ and His Good News (Gospel) of the Bible, "You can be saved." They are different from hymns and psalms, because they were a way of sharing the hard condition of being a slave."

Also, Pembroke is near Nortenville, Kentucky where my wife, Joan, grew up. Joan helped supply some details of the area however, *Bettie* is *not* her life story.

Some of the characters such as Mr. Browning was her mother's dad. Miss Lucy was a second wife, and I'm told, just as sweet as she could be but not her mother's mother.

A large dinner bell fell on her and broke her hip causing her wheelchair confinement the remainder of her life. I'm told she did in fact make the best dried, fried apple pies. Hopefully my depiction of them are in good taste.

Other characters such as Mr. Teague and all the men who dressed as Indians are relatives but their part in the story is in no way a reflection of their character. I simply used some of Joan's family names to make the story more authentic and realistic for the area.

The Johnson family is completely fictitious.

If any of her family reads my story about them and doesn't like having their family name used I might get shot by one of the clan.

I hope you have enjoyed Bettie's story in "Secrets of Silvercreek" and will read its sequel, "Seasons of Separation."

Other books by the author:

Miss Lucy's recipe for Dried Fried Apple Pie:

Peal, core and quarter apples. Then slice into thin layers to be dried. Can be dried in the sun on a rack or in a stove oven.
Or buy at grocery store.

Directions for 2 people:
Reconstitute one cup of dried apples in pan, add 1/2 half cup of water. Let set for 20 minutes. Turn on heat to cook apples, add cinnamon and sugar to taste. Just a pinch of salt to bring out flavor.

Roll pie dough out thin as can be worked with. Place half the cooked apples on one side of the dough and fold the other half over the apples and crimp edges together.

Place in hot, greased skillet. Turn as each side is cooked.
(Hint) Use two spatulas to turn tender dough in skillet.
Set out on paper towels to dry and cool.
Enjoy.

Miss Lucy's recipe for Fried Squirrel:

    Get Mr. Browning and his ole dog 'Baccer Worm' to hunt you some squirrels. After Mr. Browning skins the hide off of them wash and soak the cut up pieces in salt water. Roll them in flour and then fry them until they are tender and crispy like fried chicken.

Miss Lucy's recipe for Boiled Okra:

    Take fresh okra pods picked from the garden and wash them good in cold water—it'll make the baccer worms crawl out and not get cooked.
    After the pods are cleaned place them in a pan of water to boil until the pods are tender. They are ready to eat, if you can stand the slime.
